"Stop it, Lux," Patrick commanded. "I won't be one of your causes. Stop hovering over me like a mother hen!"

"Well, excuse me," she said, rising from her chair.

Patrick trapped her hand on the top of the table, forcing her to sit back down. He leaned toward her, a muscle pulsing in his jaw.

"My *needs*," he said, stressing the word, "run in a different direction. I need to kiss you, hold you, touch you. I need to make love to you until I'm too exhausted to move. I don't want to be just your friend, Lux. I won't be."

"I'm not sure what you mean," she whispered.

"There's something happening between us, Lux, that is not, definitely not, friendship in its purest form. Yes, lovers can be friends, too, but that is not what this is about. Understand?"

Lux nodded, her eyes wide, her heart pounding wildly.

He looked fierce. "I'm not going to ravish you, but what I'm saying is that we deserve a chance to find out what we're feeling means. Give us that chance, Lux, please?" he asked, pulling her up and into his arms.

She trembled as he began trailing kisses down her throat. "Yes . . . but Patrick—"

"Shh," he said. Then he kissed her lips as if he'd never let her go. . . .

WHAT ARE *LOVESWEPT* ROMANCES?

They are stories of true romance and touching emotion. We believe those two very important ingredients are constants in our highly sensual and very believable stories in the *LOVESWEPT* line. Our goal is to give you, the reader, stories of consistently high quality that may sometimes make you laugh, sometimes make you cry, but are always fresh and creative and contain many delightful surprises within their pages.

Most romance fans read an enormous number of books. Those they truly love, they keep. Others may be traded with friends and soon forgotten. We hope that each *LOVESWEPT* romance will be a treasure—a "keeper." We will always try to publish

LOVE STORIES YOU'LL NEVER FORGET
BY AUTHORS YOU'LL ALWAYS REMEMBER

The Editors

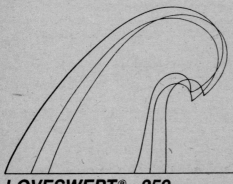

LOVESWEPT® • 259
Joan Elliott Pickart
Warm Fuzzies

 BANTAM BOOKS
TORONTO • NEW YORK • LONDON • SYDNEY • AUCKLAND

WARM FUZZIES
A Bantam Book / June 1988

LOVESWEPT® and the wave device are registered
trademarks of Bantam Books. Registered in U.S. Patent
and Trademark Office and elsewhere.

If you would be interested in receiving protective vinyl
covers for your Loveswept books, please write to this address
for information:

Loveswept
Bantam Books
P.O. Box 985
Hicksville, NY 11802

ISBN 0-553-21902-2

Published simultaneously in the United States and Canada

Bantam Books are published by Bantam Books, a division
of Bantam Doubleday Dell Publishing Group, Inc. Its trademark, consisting of the words "Bantam Books" and the
portrayal of a rooster, is Registered in U.S. Patent and
Trademark Office and in other countries. Marca Registrada.
Bantam Books, 666 Fifth Avenue, New York, New York 10103.

PRINTED IN THE UNITED STATES OF AMERICA

O   0 9 8 7 6 5 4 3 2 1

For my daughter, Robin,
who loves
rainbows, and teddy bears, and warm fuzzies

This one is for you, Rob

One

Lux Sherwood drummed her fingers on the steering wheel in time to the lively music playing on the van's radio. She glanced in the rearview mirror to see an open Jeep pulling up next to her in the heavy Phoenix rush-hour traffic.

"Hey, beautiful," a young man called from the passenger seat of the Jeep, "if your buddy there doesn't cut it, give me a call."

"Your friend is a dud, gorgeous," the driver of the Jeep yelled. "I'm a real man, just what you need."

Lux laughed in delight, gave the pair a thumbs-up sign, then watched as they sped up and crisscrossed the lanes ahead of her until they disappeared from view. She glanced over at her traveling companion, who was staring straight ahead, the harness-style seatbelt keeping him securely in place.

The comments from the occupants of the Jeep weren't the first Lux had had since beginning her drive on the freeway, but then, she reasoned, it wasn't every day of the week that she was accompanied by such an unusual passenger.

Not everyone, she admitted, drove blissfully along while sharing the cab of a van with a six-foot, royal blue teddy bear.

"That's okay, Teddy," she said, reaching over to pat the stuffed toy on the head. "I think you're the best looking guy I've seen all day."

Lux flicked on the blinker and took the next exit ramp off the freeway. From the address written on the piece of paper next to her on the seat, she knew she was headed for one of the plush homes nestled in the hills of Camelback Mountain.

"You're going to be living in style, Teddy," she said cheerfully. "You'll have to remember all of your social graces in the home of . . ." She glanced at the paper again. ". . . one Patrick Mullaney."

Patrick Mullaney jerked awake at the pealing of the doorbell. He waited to hear the sound of his housekeeper answering the summons, remembered she'd gone to the grocery store, then swore under his breath as the doorbell rang again. He reached for the pair of crutches lying on the floor next to the soft leather chair where he was sprawled, then leveled himself rather clumsily to his feet.

He made his way out of the den and down the hall, the tight Ace bandage wrapping his knee, part of his calf and thigh, keeping his right leg bent and off the ground.

His progress was slow. The doorbell rang again.

"Hell," he said. "Keep your shirt on. This had better be worth the trip."

Patrick moved to one side, leaned forward to twist the knob, staggered, then threw the door open.

As the door opened, so did his mouth.

Standing on his front porch was an enormous, grinning, royal blue teddy bear.

"What in the . . ." Patrick started, his gaze raking over the furry stuffed creature.

Wrapped around the bear's middle was a pair of arms, connected to small feminine hands. And peeking from beneath the toy's armpit was a blue eye, fringed in long, dark lashes.

"Patrick Mullaney?" a muffled voice said.

"Yeah, but . . ."

"Delivery, sir."

"You've got the wrong Patrick Mullaney," he said gruffly. "That thing doesn't belong to me."

"Could we discuss this inside?" came the mumbled reply. "You have no idea how heavy Teddy is."

"I suppose," Patrick said, shifting backward on the crutches. "Come on in, but I'm telling you, you've got the wrong place."

Lux lumbered forward with her cargo, still peering beneath the bear's arm. So far, she knew that Patrick Mullaney was not a little boy who was thrilled out of his mind over the arrival of a huge, blue bear in all its magnificent splendor. She also knew that Patrick Mullaney had an extremely masculine, nicely muscled bare chest covered in tawny curls. Patrick Mullaney was also, she deduced, in a rotten mood.

Lux heaved Teddy forward and managed to shove him around so his back was to the wall, then slid him to a sitting position. After giving Teddy an affectionate pat on the nose, she turned to face Patrick Mullaney with a bright smile on her face.

This, Lux reaffirmed in her mind, was *not* a little boy.

This was a man; a gorgeous specimen of the male gender. This was wide shoulders, tanned arms with ropy muscles, and large hands that gripped the handles of the crutches. This was a flat stomach, faded jogging shorts, and muscles-on-muscles thighs and calves. This was tousled, sun-streaked, light brown hair, yummy brown eyes, and rugged, handsome bronzed features, complete with the most sensuous lips she'd ever seen.

Oh, yes, *this was a man*!

Who was definitely not happy.

And who looked . . . probably wishful thinking on her part, Lux decided . . . vaguely familiar.

"Well, hi," she said, smiling to beat the band. "Shall I close the door for you? Certainly." She slammed the door. "Congratulations, Mr. Mullaney. You have just received an original Warm Fuzzy as your new friend."

"A warm fuzzy," Patrick repeated slowly, "as my new friend." His frown deepened. "You've got a screw loose, kid."

"I'm *not* a kid," Lux said, planting her hands on her hips.

She had a point there, Patrick thought, as he lazily scrutinized her. She was maybe five-feet-five, compared to his, and the idiotic bear's, six feet. There were shapely breasts pushing against her pale pink blouse, and womanly curves beneath those white slacks. Pretty eyes—blue, dark blue—almost the color of the dumb bear, and her features were lovely, very nice. He liked her black shoulder-length shiny hair, which swung naturally when she moved her head. So, yeah, okay, she wasn't a kid.

"Right," he said. "You're not a kid."

Her entire body knew that, Lux thought, resisting the urge to check her pulse. When Patrick Mullaney looked someone over, he really did a thorough job. She felt as though he'd peeled off her clothes one piece at a time. Which was extremely rude. And which had caused the most startling heat to curl somewhere deep within her and travel throughout her with insistent little fingers.

She cleared her throat. "Mr. Mullaney, I am Lux Sherwood, owner of Warm Fuzzies and Friends. You have just received a Warm Fuzzy, custom-made especially for you per the request of your sister, Mrs. Megan Mayne."

"Oh, Lord," Patrick said, shaking his head, "I should have known."

"The only requirement for having a Warm Fuzzy as your friend is that you must . . ." A bubble of laughter escaped from Lux's lips. She tried not to laugh, she really did, but the absurdity of the situation suddenly struck her. ". . . you must give it a big bear hug every day," she rushed on.

And then she fell apart.

She laughed until she had to wrap her arms around her aching stomach, and tears glistened in her eyes. She laughed until she glanced at Patrick Mullaney's face, and then she stopped.

"Oh," she said weakly, then took a deep breath. "Sorry. I guess you're not into hugging big blue teddy bears."

"I was," Patrick said, a slow smile tugging at his lips, "but I had to give it up. People were starting to talk." His smile widened. "You know what I mean?"

Lux matched his smile, instantly deciding that, for Patrick Mullaney, smiling was a lethal weapon. He had gleaming white teeth and his eyes turned to rich pools that looked like melted chocolate. His stern rugged features softened, and she realized he wasn't more than thirty or thirty-one, compared to her own twenty-five years old. He was, indeed, a handsome man. Who still looked familiar.

"D I know you?" she said. "Oh, forget that. Wh corny thing to say. Well, I must be going. I he u enjoy your bear. His name is Teddy, but you ca change it if you prefer."

"Wait a minute," Patrick said. "You can't leave it sitting there, and I'm not exactly able to pick it up."

"Where would you like me to put him?" Lux asked.

"Bring it in the den, I guess," he said, starting down the hall.

Lux moved to lift the bear off of the floor, then hesitated as Patrick passed her. She watched the fascinating ripple of the muscles in his tanned back, shoulders, and arms, as he swung himself forward on his crutches. Her gaze slid lower to his buttocks and powerful legs.

"Shame on me, Teddy," she whispered to the toy as she pulled her eyes from the enticing view. She hoisted the bear up, peering under its arm again, and followed Patrick down the hall.

The den was large, furnished in heavy dark furniture, and had a giant-sized television screen and an entire wall devoted to bookshelves.

"Why don't you put it on the sofa," Patrick said. He lowered himself gingerly into the leather chair, then lifted his bandaged leg onto the matching stool.

Lux shoved the bear onto a brown and orange tweed sofa. "There. You're all set, Teddy. That is one heavy bear, let me tell you."

Patrick's gaze slid over her again. "I'd say it weighs more than you do."

"Close," she said, turning to face him. "Your sister thought it might cheer you up. She said her brother had recently had an operation on his knee and . . . well, I assumed you were a bit . . . younger. She said it had to be royal blue because that is your favorite color."

"It *was* my favorite color," he said tightly.

"You changed your mind about your favorite color?"

"It was changed for me. Never mind. Would you do me a favor? My housekeeper went to the store. Would you go into the kitchen and get me a root beer? I'll drink it from the can."

"Oh, well, sure. Where's the kitchen?"

"Straight down the hall."

"I'll right back," she said, starting across the room.

"Lux?"

"Yes?" she said, stopping to look at him.

"Do you have time to join me? I could use some company. You have a very pretty name, by the way."

"Thank you. I was named after my grandmother. And, yes, I guess I have time for a cool drink."

"Good."

As Lux left the room, Patrick leaned his head back and closed his eyes with a weary sigh. His knee was throbbing like a thousand toothaches, he thought. He guessed he'd have to take the painkillers the doc had given him so he could sleep, but he'd be damned if he'd dope himself up during the day. He'd talk to Lux, maybe that would divert his attention from the fire in his leg.

Lux, he mused. He really liked that name. Pretty.

And Lux was pretty; fresh, not globbed up with tons of makeup. Her laughter was real, too—a happy sound.

He opened his eyes, glanced at the bear, and shook his head. Megan was nuts, but she meant well. It was a cute bear, actually. It was the biggest he'd ever seen. And royal blue with a big white bow around its neck. Blue and white.

"Yeah, well," he said, closing his eyes again, "you win some, you lose some." And this time, he knew, he'd lost it all. Everything.

As Lux came back down the hall, she decided that she liked Patrick Mullaney's house. It was big, bright, and sunny, obviously furnished with the best, but still had a homey, welcoming atmosphere.

And Patrick Mullaney? What did she think of him? Besides the fact that he was gorgeous, of course. She'd excuse his crabby mood because, after all, he was probably in pain from the knee surgery. Anyone who liked root beer couldn't be all bad. Beyond that, she didn't know anything about him at all. Except that she could swear she'd seen him somewhere before.

Lux reentered the den, then stopped. Patrick had his eyes closed, his head back, and she thought perhaps he'd fallen asleep. She inched closed to the chair where he sat, now seeing the fatigue etched on his face, the white line of pain around his mouth. His thick, light brown hair had tumbled onto his tanned forehead, and he looked young, and tired, and extremely vulnerable.

Lux's heart did a funny little flip-flop as she stared at him. He was so big, so strong, but at the moment he appeared all worn out, in need of comfort and protection. More comfort than could be gained by hugging a gigantic blue teddy bear, even if it was a custom-made Warm Fuzzy.

She glanced at the bandage on his knee, and wondered what had happened to him. Her gaze went further, to a row of framed pictures on the far wall, and she moved forward for a better look. As she scrutinized each photograph, her eyes widened.

Of course! she thought. That was why Patrick Mullaney looked familiar. He was Acer Mullaney, the quarterback for the Phoenix Blue Falcons football team. They'd won the Super Bowl in January. It had been a fantastic game and . . . Acer Mullaney had been hurt! In the fourth quarter he'd been sacked, his leg twisted beneath him as he'd been pounded into the ground by the defensive line that had broken through and gotten to him. She'd read in the paper that he'd just had a second operation on his knee. Now, in early April, it was still unknown if he'd ever be able to play football again.

"May I have my root beer?" Patrick asked, his voice low.

Lux spun around. "I thought you were asleep." She crossed the room and handed him a can, then settled next to the bear on the sofa with her own drink. "You're Acer Mullaney."

"Yep," he said, then took several deep swallows from the can.

"I'm sorry about your knee, but I imagine you're tired of people saying that."

"Yep." He drained the can, then overhanded it toward a wastebasket. "Two," he said, as the can landed on target. "Maybe I'll take up basketball.

No, guess not." He looked at Lux. "So, Lux Sherwood, tell me everything I ever wanted to know about Warm Fuzzies and Friends."

"No," she said, then took a sip of root beer.

"No? Why not?"

"Because it's too important to me, too special to discuss casually. I realize you want someone to chat with for a while to take your mind off your troubles and the pain you're probably suffering. That's fine." She paused. "Read any good books lately?"

Patrick appeared rather startled, then smiled. "Somebody write that down. A woman who doesn't want to talk about herself. But I wouldn't mind hearing about this business of yours. I'm serious."

Lux narrowed her eyes and studied him for a long moment. "Well, all right. My grandmother raised me and taught me how to make stuffed toys when I was a little girl. Warm Fuzzy is my patented name for my teddy bears. Warm Fuzzies and Friends is the store I have in Scottsdale. I make other kinds of animals besides bears. Those are the 'friends.' "

"Your grandmother must be pleased, very proud of you."

"She . . . she died last year. She made me promise I'd use her insurance money to open the store. I'd been working out of the house I shared with her up until then. I'm doing very well, my reputation for excellence is growing. I take a great deal of pride in what I've accomplished. But then, I'm sure you have the same feeling about your career, too."

Patrick shrugged, a frown settling on his face.

"Or maybe you don't," Lux said, getting to her feet. "You've certainly brought a great deal of pleasure to people's lives as they watched you play over the years. Acer Mullaney. The Ace. The one who aced so many games in college, it earned you the nickname and the Heisman Trophy. Those are a lot of years you're shrugging off there, Patrick Mullaney. Well, it was nice meeting you. Good luck, and enjoy Teddy. I'll let myself out." She crossed the room to the doorway of the den.

"Lux."

She stopped and turned slightly to look back at Patrick. "Yes?"

"Teddy is a helluva fine bear."

"Thank you."

Their gaze held, a room apart yet . . . something was there, pulling them closer and closer together, although neither had moved. There was a sharper awareness crackling through the air, an unspoken message of sexuality—a woman, a man, seeing, sensing all that the other was. One Lux. One Patrick.

Lux was the first to break the spell. "Good-bye, Acer," she said softly, then hurried out the door.

"See ya," Patrick said to the empty room. He slowly switched his gaze from the doorway to the huge blue teddy bear. "So, tell me, Teddy, do you play gin rummy?" Did Lux play gin rummy? he wondered. Ah, hell, forget it. He'd never see her again, anyway.

There was no big, smiling blue teddy bear to keep Lux company during the drive home. Nor was there peppy music coming from the radio in the van since she'd turned it off.

She was alone with her thoughts.

But she wasn't alone at all.

Because Patrick "Acer" Mullaney was there.

Lux gave up her attempt to chase Patrick from her mind, because he refused to budge. She replayed in her head every word they had exchanged.

She was rattled, off-kilter. Patrick had managed to touch a place deep within her. A dark, secret place that held the essence of her femininity. His roaming chocolate eyes had missed no detail of her inside or out, it would seem, and because of his perusal she was acutely more aware of *herself*. How absurd. How strange. How exciting . . . and rather frightening.

"Enough," Lux said, smacking the steering wheel with her hand. "Go away, Acer Mullaney."

Lux left the freeway and reduced her speed as she drove across town to the middle-class suburb where she'd lived with her grandmother all of her life. Gran had loved that big old house, and Lux could still feel her presence in every room.

She thought, with a smile, that Gran would have liked Patrick Mullaney. Her grandmother would have given Lux a knowing wink after getting a glimpse of Patrick's marvelous physique, then clucked in sympathy over Patrick's injury. But not for long. No, Gran would have told him to follow the doctor's orders, then make the best of whatever turn life had decided he had to take. Lux missed her.

Lux sighed as she stopped at a red light. She was getting a case of the gloomies, she admitted, and that would never do. Things were going great. Warm Fuzzies and Friends was showing an ever-increasing profit, and her reputation was growing steadily. She had the store of her dreams, good friends, money in the bank. The future looked bright, challenging . . . but something was missing. There was a niggling little void, something that wasn't quite right.

"Would you stop it?" she said, to her image in the rearview mirror.

The driver behind her honked, and Lux jumped in surprise as she saw that the light had turned green. She sped up and waved to the man behind her.

She should be counting her blessings, Lux admonished herself, not trying to figure out what she *didn't* have. She even had her good health, which was more than she could say for Patrick Mullaney. Patrick. There he was again, front row center in her mind. But heavens, he was in a rough place. He'd been the highest ranking quarterback in the entire football league, and in one bone-crunching moment his entire life had changed. He was suffering physical pain, and must be enduring immeasurable mental anguish as he waited and wondered if his playing days were over.

Lux wrinkled her nose. There she'd sat, she mused, initially refusing to tell Patrick about her company because she hadn't liked his attitude. That had been rude on her part, not like her at all. People asked her about Warm Fuzzies and Friends all of the time, and there had even been a magazine article done on her that had brought in tons of orders.

Then why, she wondered, had she held back at first, not wanting to share it all with Patrick? Yes, okay, she hadn't felt he'd really been interested, had only been killing time to take his mind off his troubles. But so what? Why had it mattered that he should really, *really*, want to know about her company?

Lux sighed again as she replayed that moment

in Patrick's den. She hadn't wanted to tell him then, she admitted to herself, because Warm Fuzzies and Friends was very important and special to her. And in that fleeting second when she'd refused to tell Patrick about it, she'd wanted him to be listening, really listening, to what she said, caring about her and what she'd accomplished. She'd shrugged off the strange emotion and told him anyway, but how unsettling to have felt that way even for a quick beat of time.

Maybe she was working too hard, Lux considered. There was no reason on earth why Patrick Mullaney should have had such an unusual, jarring effect on her. And no reason why he should be so . . . there . . . in that van as though he'd settled into the spot vacated by Teddy.

She dated good looking men all the time. But none, she conceded, not one among them, had stirred that new, wondrous heat deep within her. None made her so infinitely glad she was a woman. None caused her to fantasize about what it would be like to be held in their strong arms, kissed by their sensuous lips. In short, none was Acer Mullaney.

"Oh, for Pete's sake," Lux said, shaking her head. She was acting so childish. She was panting after the quarterback like an adolescent in high school. A quarterback who was hurt and vulnerable. A quarterback who had evoked desire within her by simply looking at her with his incredible brown eyes. A quarterback with a nonstop body and a smile to match. A quarterback, she told herself firmly, she was never going to see again, so she was dusting him out of her brain space *now*. This very minute.

With a decisive nod, Lux pulled into the driveway and turned off the ignition. She slid off the seat and out the door and glanced with pride at the brightly colored lettering on the side of the white van. WARM FUZZIES AND FRIENDS it said. Her dream. Hours and hours of back-breaking labor had paid off. Everything was terrific.

Except for that niggling little void that . . .

"Don't start that again," she mumbled, going to the rear of the van.

She retrieved a box of small stuffed toys that would be her hand sewing for the evening, walked across the grass, and up onto the long front porch. The window next to the door was raised and a dark, curly head popped out, followed by the top half of a good looking man in his mid-twenties.

"Hi, Lux," he said. "We're still on the waiting list for three different locksmiths to fix that jammed dead bolt."

"Wonderful," she said, walking over to him. She handed him the box. "Did anyone figure out how to get the back door unstuck? Paint is paint, not Super Glue, Mick."

"Nope. It won't budge. We're trying to come up with a plan. Climb in here. Pete and I made spaghetti sauce that's out of this world."

Lux laughed. "We've been crawling in and out of this window for four days now. I wonder what the neighbors think."

"That we're all crazy. Come on in."

Lux climbed inside and glanced around and saw that, as usual, the house was spotlessly clean. The delicious aroma of spices wafted through the air. She closed her eyes and took a deep breath.

"Delicious," she said. "I'll change my clothes and be right back. Is Sally here?"

"She's resting," Mick said. "She doesn't look

good, Lux. Her ankles and feet are swollen like you wouldn't believe. Pete and I were talking about it. We think Sally should quit her job as a waitress right now. Pete and I will kick in extra to make up her share."

Lux smiled at him. "You two are really sweet. But I told Sally last week that she should quit working, and that it didn't matter about her paying for the room for now. I wanted it to be my gift to her and the baby, but she said no. She has a month to go before that baby is due, and I don't think she should be on her feet so much. She said she's lucky to have a boss who will keep her on looking like a blimp . . . her word, not mine. I'll talk to her again, though."

"Good. Lux, do you think Sally should be so fat?"

She laughed. "She's having a baby, Mickey."

"I know, but she nearly got stuck climbing in the window. How big can one little baby be?"

"The doctor says she's fine," Lux said. "Where's Pete?"

"Call my name," a tall, thin, handsome, blond man said, coming out of the kitchen, "and I come on command."

"How nice," Lux said, smiling. "I'll be right back to sample your spaghetti."

"Hustle up," Pete said. "Mick and I have to go earn our keep, play our music, peel the women from our bodies when the evening is over."

"Oh, spare me," Lux said. She crossed the room.

"It's true," Mick called after her. "Groupies. Pete and I have groupies. Oodles and oodles of groupies."

"We do?" Pete said.

"Well, we will," Mick said, "when we hit the big time. Hear that, Lux? We're hitting the big time!"

Lux laughed softly as she went down the hall to her room and closed the door. She sincerely hoped that Mick and Pete did make it big. They had talent, dedication, and they deserved the musical success they sought. She wanted to see them awe the country, and never have anything happen to shatter their world as hers had . . .

"Patrick," she said aloud, pulling on faded jeans. There he was again, filling her thoughts. This was nuts, it really was. Patrick "Acer" Mullaney was a man like any other. Well, that was stretching it a bit. He had definitely been dished out an extra serving of all the ingredients that went into creating the male species. Ingredients. Recipe. Food. Spaghetti. She was hungry, that's all. Once her stomach was full and she'd put her feet up to relax, she'd regain control of her wayward thoughts.

Dinner, as usual, was a boisterous affair. The spaghetti proved to be as delicious as promised, the conversation was lively.

"I . . . um . . . delivered a Warm Fuzzy to Acer Mullaney today," Lux said casually, reaching for a breadstick.

"Sure you did," Pete said. "And tomorrow you'll take one to Don Johnson."

"Tom Selleck," Sally said. "I adore his mustache."

"I *did* go to Acer Mullaney's," Lux said. "I was in his house, his den, his kitchen. I brought him a root beer from his refrigerator."

"I'll be damned," Mick said. "How's his knee doing? The Blue Falcons are going to be in very bad shape if they lose Acer. How did he look?"

Gorgeous. "He's on crutches," Lux said. Why had she done this to herself? Why in heaven's name had she brought up the subject of Patrick Mullaney when she'd managed to go ten whole minutes without thinking about him? "He didn't say much about his knee."

"I sure hope he can play again," Pete said.

"No joke," Mick said. "He's the best quarterback in the league. Or was, before he got creamed."

"Those sports doctors work miracles," Lux said. "Surely they can help him. He's young, healthy, in terrific shape, and—"

"Oh?" Mick said, grinning at her. "Checked him out, did you?"

"Of course, she did," Sally said. "I saw Acer Mullaney's picture on the cover of *People* magazine. He's Hollywood material, folks. What a hunk of stuff! Even if he can't play football anymore, he'd have a zillion other things to pick from."

"Yeah. I guess," Mick said, "but the guy obviously loves the sport. It would be a shame if the decision to retire wasn't his to make. He also loves the ladies, from what I hear. He has a different luscious beauty on his arm all the time. More power to him. At least there's never any hint that he's into drugs or booze like some of those high rollers. Who sent him a Warm Fuzzy, Lux?"

"His sister," she said. "Acer Mullaney is a ladies' man?"

"So they say," Mick said, with a shrug. "Who could blame him? He's got it all; looks, build, fame, and fortune."

"And a bummed-up knee," Pete said.

" 'Tis true," Mick said. "That's life for you. One minute everything is hunky-dory then . . . Oh, well, so it goes. We'd better shove off, Pete. I love the rules of this place: Whoever cooks doesn't have to clean up. It allows me to expand my creative juices in the kitchen, really create culinary art."

"He's trying to say," Sally said, "that they used every pot and pan again."

Mick and Pete smiled as they got to their feet.

" 'Bye, y'all," Mick said. "If any of my fans call, take messages."

" 'Bye," Lux said absently. She glanced over to see the pair climb through the window, then reach back in for their guitars. "The neighbors must be loving this."

"Oh, I'm so full," Sally said, pressing her hands to her well-rounded stomach.

"The spaghetti was great," Lux said. "I don't remember reading that Acer Mullaney had gobs of women. How did I miss that?"

"Is he really good looking in person?" Sally said.

"Really," Lux said, nodding.

"And you were in his house," Sally said, with a sigh. "You lucky duck. Do you think he'd like a nineteen-year-old, unwed whale?"

"You don't look like a whale," Lux said, "but speaking of said baby, you and I are going to have a chat while you put your feet up and I clean the kitchen."

"No, I'll do my share."

"Sally, you're outnumbered. I'm speaking for Mick and Pete, too. Now, mother-to-be, you listen to me . . ."

A little over an hour later, Lux and Sally were settled in the living room, each hand sewing the stuffed toys as they watched an old movie on television. To Lux's relief, she'd convinced Sally to give notice at the café where she worked. Lux had asked Sally to pay for her room and board by helping with the hand work needed on all products from Warm Fuzzies and Friends. Sally had sewn for Lux in the past during peak rush times and the young girl's work was excellent. Sally had wept with gratitude, hugs had been exchanged, then they'd gotten busy on the boxful of toys Lux had brought home.

Sally's situation was only temporarily under control, Lux knew. They all were avoiding the topic of what Sally would do once the baby was born. How would she support herself and raise a child? What would a baby in the house do to the routine of the others living there? The questions were going to have to be faced, Lux realized, and soon.

The telephone rang, rescuing Lux from her tangled thoughts, and she answered it with a rather mumbled greeting.

" 'Lo?"

"Lux?"

"Yes."

"This is Acer Mullaney . . . Patrick."

Lux sat bolt upright on the sofa, then glanced quickly at Sally, who wasn't paying the least bit of attention to her.

Stay calm, Lux told herself frantically. The man didn't know he'd been doing an instant replay in her mind ever since she'd left his house. She could handle this. She'd be cool, sophisticated, ultra-mature.

"Lux? Are you there?"

"Who? Oh, yes, I'm here. You betcha," she said. Oh, for crying out loud!

"Listen, I've got a real problem here, emergency status, red alert."

Lux's eyes widened. "What's wrong?"

"It's Teddy. There's been a terrible accident."

"Teddy . . . Huh?"

"Okay, here it is. I fell asleep in the den, and it was pretty dark in there. My housekeeper fixed me some dinner and brought it to me on a tray. Maria, that's my housekeeper, came into the den, set the tray on the table, then saw the outline of Teddy sitting in the shadows on the sofa. He scared the bejeebers out of her."

"Oh, dear," Lux said.

"Anyway, she picked up the first thing that she put her hand on and threw it at Teddy, thinking he was a burglar or whatever. She was screaming her head off. I nearly killed myself coming out of that chair."

"Oh, dear," Lux said. "What did she throw at him?"

"The bottle of catsup she'd brought in to go with my hamburger and fries. You should see Teddy. He's a mess, looks like he's bleeding to death. You have to help me, Lux. If Megan sees him like this, she'll be really upset. You wouldn't want my sister to be upset, would you? No, of course not. So, what time?"

Lux blinked. "What time what?"

"Are you coming over tomorrow to help restore Teddy to his original dashing self?"

Two

At ten o'clock the next morning, Lux stood on Patrick Mullaney's front porch, staring at the closed door, and wondering what on earth she was doing there.

She had explained to Patrick that the card attached to the white bow around Teddy's neck not only explained that the bear required a hug a day, but also gave instructions for cleaning the Warm Fuzzy should it become necessary.

Patrick, however, had pleaded his case. Maria was still in a state of shock, Megan would be crushed if she saw Teddy appearing as though he'd been attacked by an ax murderer, and Lux just had to come to Patrick's rescue.

"My bear looks like the victim of a war!" Patrick had yelled, and Lux had dissolved in a fit of laughter. Sally, by then, was definitely paying close attention to the conversation.

Somewhere in the midst of all that, Lux mused, she'd agreed to come to Patrick's at ten the next morning. Why? That question had bounced around in her brain for half the night.

But, now, standing there staring at Patrick's intricately carved front door, there was no way to escape the truth. She was there, Lux knew, because she wanted to see Patrick "Acer" Mullaney again.

It was as simple as that.

No, she corrected herself, it was as complicated as that.

She, Lux Sherwood, had driven clear across town to see a man? Ludicrous. Based on the harebrained premise that her expertise was needed to scrub catsup off an enormous, blue teddy bear, she was now at said man's house? Ridiculous. Granted, Warm Fuzzies and Friends was in the capable hands of her assistant, Sharon, but still . . . this was really absurd!

Well, now that she was here, she'd just breeze in, using the professional decorum of a doctor making a house call, tend to the situation, then make a quick exit.

She would not, Lux instructed herself, gawk at Patrick's gorgeous body, or gaze into his magnificent eyes. She would not fall prey to his overwhelming masculinity, nor to the underlying vulnerability caused by his injury. But she *would* remember her newly discovered information that Patrick Mullaney was a ladies' man, and she'd stay alert. There. She'd covered all the bases. Now, all she had to do was raise her hand and knock on the door.

She didn't move.

"Quit acting like a dolt, Sherwood," she said aloud.

She knocked lightly, very lightly, on the door. In the next instant it was flung open, and Lux jumped in surprise.

"Hi," Patrick said, smiling. "I wondered how long you were going to stand out there. I saw your van pull in, then . . . nothing. I thought maybe you were meditating or something."

Lux was totally mortified and felt a warm flush on her cheeks. She just wanted to crawl into a hole and die. Talk about embarrassing.

"I . . ." She cleared her throat. ". . . had a knot in my shoelace."

Patrick's gaze slid over her face, her lightweight, short-sleeve, red sweater, down her jean-clad legs to land at last on her tennis-shoe-covered feet, complete with shoelaces. Heat churned within Lux at the slow scrutiny, and she frowned.

O-kay, Mullaney, she thought. She could play this game, too.

When his gaze returned to her face, having traveled back up with the same agonizing slowness as it had gone down, she looked at him, at his chocolate-colored eyes, and smiled. Then, oh, so very slowly she shifted her attention to his tanned features, on to broad shoulders covered in a green knit shirt, then lower. She drifted down to his wide chest, flat stomach, narrow hips. Faded cut-offs hugged muscled thighs, then on she went to one bandaged knee, and two muscled calves. By the time she got to tattered tennies with no socks, her heart was dancing a jig, and she was sure there wasn't an ounce of breath left in her body. She forced herself to retrace her visual steps to look at Patrick's face again.

He was grinning at her, merriment dancing in his eyes. "Touché," he said. "I definitely feel like beef on the hoof. Your point, Ms. Sherwood. Won't you come in?"

"Thank you," she said, ever so politely, totally amazed that she could speak.

Patrick hopped backward on his crutches and Lux moved past him with, she hoped, a smug expression on her face. Patrick's low, sexy chuckle did nothing to settle her still wildly thudding heart.

"The patient is still in the den," Patrick said.

"Of course," Lux said, then started down the hall.

Patrick's smile grew bigger as he shook his head, then hobbled after her. Lord, she was something, he thought. One minute she was actually blushing, which he didn't think women did anymore, and in the next minute she was acting all huffy and poking her nose in the air. He adored her hair, liked to watch the dark swirl as it swung freely when she tossed her head. Oh, yeah, she was something.

But even more, he thought, she was there. He hadn't been able to get her off his mind after she'd left the day before. He'd remembered every word they'd exchanged, could recall her laughter, smile, the delicate scent of a light, feminine cologne. He'd been startled by her lingering presence since Lux Sherwood really wasn't his type. He went more for voluptuous blondes.

But Lux . . . Well, he'd finally admitted that she'd intrigued him, and he wanted to see her again to figure out why. It was probably due to the fact that he was bored out of his mind from sitting around staring at his knee and four walls. But when Maria had creamed Teddy with the cat-sup bottle, the opportunity to contact Lux was just too good to pass up. So, here she was, lured back into his den. Literally.

"Oh, merciful heavens," Lux said.

Patrick quickened his pace and entered the den to see Lux staring at Teddy.

"I told you it was grim," Patrick said. "I had to shuffle all the way into the kitchen for my breakfast because Maria refused to come in here. Ol' Teddy really shook her up."

Lux laughed. "I'd say that Maria held her own. What a mess. Well, it's bath time, Teddy." She looked at Patrick. "Do you have a laundry room with a sink?"

"Yeah, but it's off the kitchen. Maria's baking something in the kitchen. We'll have to use a bathroom. Mine is the biggest. I wish I could help you tote him."

"No problem," Lux said. *Oh, great*, she thought. *Just super.* Now, they were going to tromp through Patrick's bedroom to get to his bathroom. His bedroom, for heaven's sake. The place where Mr. Lady Killer . . . No, she wasn't going to think about it. After all, it had nothing to do with her. She was simply the doctor on call treating a patient. Her mind knew that. It was her body that was going slightly nuts over the prospect of entering Acer Mullaney's bedroom.

She dragged Teddy forward by one foot, then shifted him so she could catch him under the arms from behind to avoid plastering his catsup-covered front against her. His legs dragged on the floor, and she was forced to hoist him up, wrapping her arms around his sticky middle and peering under his arm as she'd done the day before to deliver him.

"Ugh," she said. "This is really gross. Lead on, Mullaney."

"Right," he said, swiveling on the crutches. "Follow me."

Anywhere, Lux thought dreamily, gazing at Patrick's buttocks. He didn't even have to blow in her ear. *Oh, Lux, knock it off this very minute.*

Patrick glanced at her for a second as they started down the hall. "What a trio," he said, smiling. "A hobbling jock, a wounded blue bear, and a beautiful woman. We should take this act on the road."

Lux stumbled slightly, then kept moving with her heavy cargo. Beautiful woman? she repeated in her mind. Her? Beautiful? Attractive, yes. Wholesome, pretty enough not to scare babies, but beautiful? Oh, now hold it. She had to remember who was calling her beautiful. This was ladies' man Mullaney. She wasn't falling for this malarkey. But . . . beautiful?

Peering under Teddy's arm she followed Patrick into his bedroom, instantly deciding that never in her life had she seen such a huge room. The king-size bed covered in an orange and brown spread hardly made a dent in the expanse. There was a long dresser and an upright bureau constructed of heavy, dark wood. One wall held a fireplace in front of which was a coffee table and two matching tweed easy chairs. The carpet beneath her feet was tan, plush, and thick.

"What a lovely room," she said. Her words were rather muffled as she spoke into Teddy's furry back. Big bed, she thought. Very big bed. Very big, busy bed. Oh, stop!

"The bathroom is through here," Patrick said, moving on.

"Good gracious," Lux said, when she entered the bathroom. "That's not a bathtub, it's a swimming pool."

"It's a spa, hot tub thing. After a rough game it feels like heaven. All those warm jets of water are like a woman's soothing touch."

Do tell, Lux thought dryly. And she'd bet he'd had plenty of opportunity to compare the difference between water jets and women's hands. Or both at once. Heaven knew there was room for two in that tub. What would it be like to be worldly and sophisticated, just calmly join Patrick Mullaney in the swirling warm water of his sunken tub, then . . .

"What do we do first?" Patrick said, interrupting Lux's wayward thoughts.

"What? Oh, Teddy. Yes, of course." She slid him to the floor, then propped his back against the wall. "Soap, water, and a sponge. This material is washable and stain resistant. I'm not sure how it will do with catsup that has had all night to set, though."

"There should be a sponge under the sink. I'm not being very helpful."

"Don't worry about it. You can sit on that padded bench and supervise. Okay, Teddy, let's see what I can do about your poor battered body."

Patrick lowered himself to the bench and watched as Lux knelt and lathered the front of the bear, then began to scrub vigorously with the sponge.

Lucky bear, Patrick mused. Lux's hands were covering some very interesting territory. Yep, he could go for some of the tender lovin' care those pretty little hands were dishing out. Lux was beautiful. Her hair was swinging back and forth, he had a profile view of her breasts, bottom, legs, her pert nose. She had a natural beauty that matched the freshness of the cologne she wore.

Patrick smiled. There he sat, he thought, big time, hot shot Mullaney, watching a whisper of a woman scrub catsup off of a six-foot blue bear in his bathroom. No one would believe this nonsense. *He* hardly believed it. If he'd gotten a woman this far, she'd be in his tub by now, the warm spray working its seductive magic while they sipped champagne. What would Lux look like glowing with the heat of the water and the heat of passion? Passion created by him, and directed toward him. Man, oh, man.

Patrick shifted slightly on the bench as his body tightened from the images he was painting in his mind.

No, he decided, Lux wouldn't go for a romp in the bubbles, followed by a tumble into his bed, a one-night stand. He just somehow knew she wasn't the kind to go in for casual sex, no strings attached. She was different from the women he associated with, the ones who understood how the game was played. There was something about her that said she traveled a different road than he did. She could hold her own, as evidenced by the way she'd looked him over just as he'd done to her. But then she'd blush, or drop her gaze, and he'd see and sense the vulnerability beneath the façade.

Nope, he silently affirmed, she wasn't his type. But she sure was beautiful. And he sure as hell had knocked himself out getting her back over to his house so he could see her again. Boredom. It had to be plain, old boredom. Or . . . was it?

"Lux?" he said.

"Hmm?" she said, still scrubbing Teddy.

"I really appreciate your doing this. Is the cat-sup coming off?"

"Yes." She got to her feet, rinsed the sponge, smiled at Patrick, then got back to work. "I think Teddy is going to be as good as new."

"I'm glad somebody is," Patrick said, under his breath, glancing at his wrapped knee.

"I heard that, Patrick," Lux said, not looking at him, "but I'll pretend I didn't if you don't want to talk about your knee."

"I wish more people felt that way. The press is hounding me, hounding the doctors, the coaches. Everyone wants to know if I'll be able to play again." He paused. "Well, aren't you going to ask if I'll be able to play again?"

"No. If you wanted to tell me, you would. Be-sides, it says in the newspapers that you don't know yet."

"I know," he said quietly.

Lux looked up at him quickly, then switched her gaze back to Teddy. "Oh."

Patrick leaned his head back against the wall and closed his eyes. "There will be a press confer-ence in a couple of days," he said, his voice flat. "I'll announce my retirement then. It's all over, Lux. Finished."

Lux turned and sat down on the floor, crossing her legs Indian style. Patrick opened his eyes and met her gaze.

"So?" he said, a rough edge to his voice. "How about a few platitudes here? You know, 'I'm sorry, Acer,' or 'My God, what a rotten hand you've been dealt, Acer,' or 'My heart aches for you, Patrick.' Come on, Lux," he said, his voice rising, "lay it all on me. Tell me how I can pick and choose from a whole list of new careers. Tell me I'm young and have my entire life ahead of me, can make a place for myself somewhere else. Tell me that football is just a little boy's game played by men who never grew up, so what's the big deal, anyway. Yeah, how about some sympathy, then a good old-fashioned pep talk? That's what's called for here, you know."

"Do you . . ." Lux started, then lifted her chin, ". . . have a blow-dryer?"

"What?"

"Teddy is all cleaned. I need to blow him dry and fluffy."

"Damn you!" Patrick yelled, lunging to his feet. He gripped the towel rod for support. "Didn't you hear what I said? I'm finished as a football player, Lux!"

Lux got to her feet and ran her damp hands over her jeans. "I heard you, Patrick," she said softly. "But I can't believe that you really want platitudes from me. You're going to hear them from so many people. Right now you're angry, maybe a bit frightened, terribly upset, and I don't blame you one bit. Those are real and honest emotions, and you have every right to feel that way." She paused. "For a while. Then? Then, you're going to have to put the pieces of your life back together and, in spite of all those around you who will be pressuring you to make a decision, you and only you can really decide what you want to do."

"Lux, I—" he said.

"I'm sorry this happened to you, Patrick, but I can't change it or fix it. I can only listen if you want to talk, understand when you wish to be silent. You can rant and rave, throw things, you could even cry, and I wouldn't pass judgment on you." She moved closer to look directly up at him. "Cry, Patrick, if it will help. Work out all the emotions that are churning inside you, then take a deep breath, and get on with your life."

Patrick looked down at her, a muscle jumping along his tightly clenched jaw. His tawny brows were knit in a frown as he stared at her as though warring within himself. Anger flashed in his dark eyes, and Lux saw it, along with the pain and confusion that followed. She didn't move. She just stood statue still, meeting his tormented gaze.

"Damn," Patrick said, his voice raspy.

He slid his hand to the nape of her neck, lowered his head, and kissed her.

The kiss was rough and Lux refused to respond, refused to part her lips for his insistent tongue.

But then the kiss gentled, became soft, sensuous, coaxing, and Lux could feel some of the tension ebbing from Patrick's taut body. She parted her lips, and his tongue slipped inside her mouth to explore every dark, hidden crevice. She placed her hands lightly on his chest, knowing he was balanced precariously, one of his hands still gripping the towel rod. She met his tongue with her own, and desire swirled within her.

The taste and feel of Lux's mouth moving beneath his caused heat to gather low in Patrick's body, stirring him, causing a sweet ache. He pushed aside the anger in his mind, the fear eating at him, the pain in his knee, and concentrated only on Lux. On his want and need of Lux.

He wanted to pull her closer, press her soft curves to the entire length of his hard, heated body. He wanted to lower her to the thick rug on the floor, and remove her clothes, then his. He wanted to make love to her for hours, having all the passion he now knew she possessed directed toward him. Oh, yes, he wanted, he needed, he ached for Lux Sherwood.

Patrick raised his head a fraction of an inch. "Lux . . ." he said, his voice thick with passion.

No! his mind thundered. *No, don't say it.* He couldn't tell her that he wanted her. This was Lux, who was special and different, who didn't have quickies, or unmeaning rolls in the hay. This was Lux, who had stood up to him, looked him right in the eye and told him to go with his anger and other emotions, then be done with it. This was Lux, who wouldn't have called him weak even if he'd cried.

"Thank you, Lux Sherwood," he said quietly. "You're a helluva woman."

Lux lifted her lashes, her eyes smoky blue, nearly gray, with desire. And then she smiled. To Patrick, it was the most beautiful, most tender, most feminine smile he'd ever seen, and his heart thundered. With every bit of willpower he possessed, he straightened fully and dropped his hand from her neck. Lux took her hands from his chest.

"And I think . . ." she whispered. ". . . that you're a helluva man."

Their eyes met in a moment that could not be measured in time. The room disappeared, along with the soggy blue bear. They were apart from reality, transported to a place that was surrounded in a hazy glow, leaving space only for the two of them. Heat seemed to weave back and forth between them, causing desire to be kindled from the glowing ember to a roaring flame.

"My God," Patrick said, his voice gritty, "what is happening here? What are you doing to me?"

Lux blinked, and the room came back into focus along with Teddy. "I . . ." she started, then had to draw air into her lungs. ". . . I don't know. I could ask you what you're doing to me, but I won't. It was a kiss, Patrick, just a kiss." *Like none other I've ever experienced in my life.*

"Was it?" he said, a husky quality to his voice. He shifted backward and settled onto the bench again, his eyes never leaving her.

"Yes, of course. It was an emotional moment. You're in a rough place in your life. I understand that."

He crossed his arms loosely over his chest. "I see."

"You do?" she said, frowning slightly. "Oh. Well, that's good."

"I see that what you just said was a bunch of bull."

Lux's eyes widened. "It was not."

"Damn right it was, lady. That kiss was real, man and woman, you and me. It had nothing to do with whether or not I'm upset about my knee, my future, my demolished bear, or the state of the economy. It was me kissing you, wanting you. It was you kissing me, wanting me. Don't jumble it together with a bunch of stuff that has nothing to do with it."

"Well! You don't have to get all in a snit about it, Patrick Mullaney. This whole conversation is insane, considering the fact that we're having it in the middle of a bathroom in the company of a giant blue bear. Do you have a blow-dryer or not? I have work to do here."

"Whew," he said, grinning at her, "that's quite a temper you've got there. The blow-dryer is in the cupboard over there."

Lux glared at him, yanked open the cupboard, and pulled out the blow-dryer, knocking over a plastic bottle in the process.

"Lilac bubblebath?" she said, straightening the bottle. "And what's this? Roses, Jasmine, Gardenias? My, my, you are prepared for all preferences, aren't you?"

"I try," he said, still smiling.

"So I've heard," she said slamming the cupboard door.

"What have you heard?" he said, his smile fading.

She shrugged. "This and that. Okay, Teddy, let's dry you off."

"Hold it. What have you heard, Lux?"

She looked at him. "That you're a ladies' man. You know, 'love 'em and leave 'em.' "

"Oh, that," he said, waving a hand in the air. "The press likes that image. They play it up for all it's worth."

"Pictures don't lie."

"Hey, I'm not denying that I like women, because I do. Women are nice, soft, they smell good. I've spent half of my life surrounded by big, mean, muscle-bound men. Women are a delightful change. That doesn't make me a rotten person."

"Whatever," Lux said, then plugged in the blow-dryer.

"Don't turn that on. Lux, I never make phony promises to women. I'm honest and upfront, and . . ."

"Patrick," she interrupted, "you don't owe me any explanation for your social conduct. Now, if you don't mind, I'd like to get Teddy dried off."

"Well, hell, you make me sound like a louse, a bed-hopping louse."

"I never said that," she said, then turned on the blow-dryer.

Patrick frowned and leaned back against the wall. Hell, he thought, so what if he had a lot of women in his life, it was none of Lux's business. Not that she exactly seemed to care one way or the other. Why didn't she care? Hadn't that kiss meant anything at all to her? That kiss had been special. It sure as hell had better have meant something to her!

He shook his head. He was cracking up, he decided, really losing it. And it was all Lux Sherwood's fault. He'd never met anyone like her before, and she was driving him nuts. He had enough problems in his life without trying to figure out a woman he didn't understand from one minute to the next.

But, oh, Lord, that kiss, he rambled on. It had really been something. There was so much passion in Lux, so much giving. And he wanted it all. He wanted to make love to her so badly. . . .

Boredom? he wondered again. Boredom, combined with the fact that he knew that she wasn't the type to have a fast romp in bed? The ol' "wanting what he couldn't have" routine? That made sense, it really did.

But . . .

But there was a strange knot in the pit of his belly that said there was more than that going on here. Oh, man, he didn't need this hassle, not now, not when his life was in the blender. He wanted Lux to dry the stupid bear, walk out of his front door, and disappear.

Didn't he?

Damn right, he did.

Didn't he?

Oh, Lord, he thought, he really was losing his mind!

Lux shut off the blow-dryer and patted Teddy. "Good as new." She looked at Patrick. "No one will ever know he was in a mighty battle."

"Thanks, Lux, I appreciate it," Patrick said. He watched as she put the blow-dryer and sponge away. "Lux?"

"Hmm?"

"Those things you said to me after I told you I'm washed up in football . . . That was heavy stuff. I can't imagine one other person I know telling me to cry if I felt the need."

"You were hearing the philosophy my grandmother raised me with, Patrick. I can remember when I was seven or eight and some kids at school had been taunting me about having only an old lady to live with instead of a real mother and father. I hit one of the kids, then ran all the way home, flung myself into Gran's arms, and cried. She said that was fine, to get it all out of my system, then realize it wasn't going to change, so I'd better accept that."

Patrick nodded.

"I heard the platitudes from time to time from people over the years. You know, 'Oh, you poor little thing, to think that your parents just up and left you,' things like that. But it was as though they were speaking to someone else, because I'd long since had my cry and made my peace, thanks to Gran."

"She sounds like a remarkable woman."

"She was, and I miss her."

"I can imagine. Lux, your parents left you?"

She shrugged. "They drove an eighteen-wheeler as a team. They had no room in their lives for a baby."

"Damn. Where are they now?"

"I have no idea. I haven't heard from them in over twenty years. They just didn't . . . need me."

"I'm sorry."

She switched her gaze to Teddy. "There's no reason to be. Now! Where do you want me to put our friend? I don't think he's too safe in the den."

"Could you put him in one of the chairs by the fireplace in the bedroom? Then I'll warn Maria that's where he is so she doesn't flip out again."

"Okay," Lux said, lifting the bear from the floor. "Here we go."

Patrick reached for the crutches and followed her out of the bathroom. Lux plopped Teddy into the chair, then straightened the bow around his neck.

Then she straightened it some more.

She was stalling, she knew it, but couldn't seem to hurry herself. There was no longer any reason to stay at Patrick's. She'd leave, and that would be that. But she didn't want to go, not yet. Why? She wasn't quite sure. The kiss? Was that it? That was definitely part of it, because it had been a wondrous kiss, a kiss like none before.

But there was more than the kiss, she admitted. She and Patrick had shared inner feelings and secrets, as though they'd known each other forever. He'd allowed the emotions about his heart-ache and fear over his shattered career to surface. She'd told him about her parents, something very few people knew. There was a bond between them that went deeper than physical attraction. It was . . . well, a warm fuzzy feeling inside of her, separate from the desire Patrick had evoked within her. No, she didn't want to leave yet, but she had to because there was no longer any plausible reason to stay.

"Well," she said, looking somewhere over Patrick's left shoulder, "I must be on my way."

Now? Patrick's mind raced. *Already?* She was leaving? "Look," he said, "I'd like to take you to lunch to thank you for fixing Teddy up, but I can't drive yet. Would you have lunch here? Maria always makes plenty. Okay?"

The warm fuzzy feeling within Lux grew, and she smiled.

"I'd be delighted, Patrick."

At midnight, Patrick sat in the dark in his bedroom in the chair opposite Teddy. The pain in his leg had driven him from the tossing and turning he'd been doing in his bed. He was, he admitted reluctantly, going to have to take a pain pill in order to get some sleep. He'd been hoping to avoid taking any more of the drug because it caused nightmares, and a rotten headache in the morning. But his knee was killing him, and the doc had stressed the importance of getting proper sleep.

Maybe, Patrick mused, he could relax his muscles and ease some of the pain if he thought about something else. For example . . . Lux. Did he want to think about Lux? Too late, there she was in his mind as clearly as though she were standing in front of him.

Beautiful, beautiful Lux.

Maria had sure liked her, Patrick recalled, even when she'd been told that it had been Lux who had made the scary blue bear. Maria had served them a delicious lunch out on the terrace, and he and Lux had chatted comfortably about all and everything: movies, books, politics, the non-stop growth of Phoenix, and on and on. It had been really nice.

Patrick frowned. Lux's parents were duds, he thought. How could they have dumped off a baby as though she were dirty laundry, then gone tooling on their way, not giving her another thought? Thank God that Lux had her grandmother to raise her. But still, he'd heard the slight tremor in Lux's voice when she'd said, "They just didn't need me," as she'd spoken of her parents. Hell, they didn't deserve someone like Lux. She was special.

A hot pain shot up Patrick's leg and he stiffened, gritting his teeth. "Damn," he said, beads of sweat dotting his upper lip. One play, one damn play that went wrong after thousands he'd called, barking out the signals to his teammates. One play that allowed human concrete walls to get through the line and sack him. One damn play, and his career was over.

Over. Finished. Done.

He was washed up, just another jock who couldn't cut it anymore. Someone else would wear his blue and white jersey, use his number, put their stuff in his locker. He'd be forgotten as though he'd never existed.

Over. Finished. Done.

"Ah, damn," Patrick said. He reached forward

and grabbed Teddy's foot, hauling the big bear out of the chair. Patrick placed his large hands on the toy's shoulders to steady Teddy in a sitting position on the floor in front of him. "Oh, man, Teddy," he said, his voice raspy, "it stinks, it really does." An achy sensation seized his throat. "I'm scared, man. Ah, hell, Teddy, what am I going to do?"

Then, there in the dark room, Patrick "Acer" Mullaney wrapped his arms around the bear's neck, buried his face in the soft blue fur on top of the toy's head . . . and cried.

Three

Warm Fuzzies and Friends was located on a pretty winding street off Scottsdale Road that housed exclusive boutiques and specialty shops. While the stores on the main street of Scottsdale were required to maintain an outward appearance of the Old West, the shops on the side streets were not.

The prestigious little town was tucked between Phoenix, Mesa, and Tempe, the home of Arizona State University. Scottsdale was a "must-see" for tourists since it was a reminder of olden Western days. Lux knew she was fortunate to have found an empty shop in Scottsdale, and while the rent was high, so was the flow of customers. Her lease stated that she could change the interior at her expense to meet her needs, and that had been her first order of business. The multitude of shelves displayed the Warm Fuzzy collection to perfection, along with all the bears' "friends." There was a small table and chairs where several bears, a rabbit, and skunk enjoyed a tea party, and a bench swing held a group of toys smiling in anticipation of a ride. A large bear sat by the front door with a sign around its neck that said PLEASE HUG ME, and children were only too happy to oblige.

Lux and Sharon changed the display in the front window often, and were making plans to show the toys in graduation caps and gowns. Lux had placed an order for caps and gowns in a wide variety of sizes and school colors from a specialty sewing shop in Phoenix. Having discovered the excellent craftsmanship done there, Lux could concentrate on the toys themselves, knowing unique outfits were available for them when she chose.

Because of the increasing demand for her product, Lux had farmed out the cutting, sewing, and stuffing of the toys. All handwork, though, which included the closing of the last seam, and the attaching of the eyes, noses, and mouths, Lux did herself.

But even with her efficient assistant, Sharon, and the work that could be sent out to experts, there hardly seemed to be enough hours in the day. There was, Lux often moaned, always paperwork to do; orders to check for materials, updates on delivery schedules, plans to make for holidays months in advance. Business was booming at Warm Fuzzies and Friends, and while Lux was sincerely grateful, she was also becoming thoroughly exhausted.

Three days after Lux had been to Patrick's to scrub the catsup off Teddy, she was sitting in her office in the rear of the store checking invoices for the first delivery of the little graduation caps and gowns.

She tossed her pen onto the papers and rubbed her aching temples with her fingertips. She closed her eyes as the soothing motion began to ease some of the tension and pain of her headache. She closed her eyes . . . and saw and thought of Patrick Mullaney.

She had not, Lux admitted, been able to push Patrick very far from her mind for any great length of time since she'd last seen him. She had relived over and over the feel of his lips on hers, and the wondrous desire that had hummed within her.

It was ridiculous, Lux told herself over and over. Ridiculous, childish, and she'd never done anything like this before in her life. The only saving grace was that at least no one knew how foolishly she was behaving. Sally had, of course, been aware of the strange telephone call Lux had received, and Lux had reluctantly told her that it was Acer Mullaney who had been on the phone. But when Sally quizzed her the next night about the trip to Acer's, Lux had managed to sound slightly bored, stating she'd scrubbed the bear and left. No big deal. Sally had been terribly disappointed. Lux had decided she deserved an Academy Award for acting.

Why? Lux asked herself, opening her eyes. Why was Patrick having this lingering effect on her? She'd conceded the fact that he was extremely handsome and virile. But men did not usually throw Lux Sherwood for a loop.

Maybe, she mused, it had to do with the circumstances under which they had met. It hadn't been a typical social scene such as a party, where everyone was at their shining best. Patrick had been on his own turf, in his home. He'd been hurt, in pain, was vulnerable. Yet, he'd managed to be warm and fun.

And, she rambled on, he'd revealed his inner

anger, frustration, and fear over the loss of his cherished football career. He'd told her what had not yet even been announced to the press: he would never play again.

Was that it? she wondered. Was the fact that Patrick had stripped himself emotionally bare in front of her the reason he was still consuming her mind? Maybe that was part of it . . . maybe. But, oh, the sensations that had surged within her when he'd kissed her were like nothing she'd ever experienced before.

"Enough," Lux said, picking up her pen as she felt a warm flush on her cheeks. Besides, she reasoned, Patrick hadn't spilled out emotions to *her*, per se. She'd be kidding herself if she thought so. Things had simply piled up on him and she'd been the one there at the time. It could just have easily been Maria, or his sister, or a football buddy who had dropped by. Patrick was no doubt embarrassed to think he'd let down his guard in front of a woman he hardly knew. Embarrassed and relieved that he would never see her again.

Lux's headache began to pound again.

The telephone on her desk rang and she eagerly snatched up the receiver, glad to direct her mental attention to someone other than Patrick "Acer" Mullaney.

"Warm Fuzzies and Friends."

"Lux?"

"Yes."

"It's Seth. How about meeting me for a drink after work at Lulu Belle's? You can help me drown my sorrows."

"My goodness, what's wrong with you?"

"Acer Mullaney just held a press conference announcing his retirement. The Blue Falcons are going to have to scramble to find a new quarter-back. Their second string man is worthless. I have season tickets on the fifty yard line for next year. To see what? Nothing. I need a drink."

"Did . . . did you see the telecast of the press conference?" Lux asked, her heart racing.

"Yeah, there's a little TV in the employee lounge here at the bank."

"How did Acer look? I mean, this has got to be very difficult for him."

"The guy had class. He made his announcement, thanked a bunch of people, then said he was going to concentrate on the therapy necessary to get his knee working again, although he knows he can never play pro ball. The reporters were hammering at him about what his future plans were, but he said he hadn't given serious thought to anything yet."

"I see."

"He was great, very poised, but you could tell it was costing him. The coach had tears in his eyes. Acer said he was spending the majority of his time with his physical therapist. Some guy named Teddy."

"What?" Lux said, sitting bolt upward in her chair. "He's spending his time with Teddy? He said that?"

"Well, yeah, those jocks usually call in the best to work one-to-one under circumstances like these. Even though Acer won't play again, he sure as hell wants his knee in the best shape as possible. He's young and has his whole life ahead of him. Why are you so shook up about this Teddy? Do you know him?"

"No, no, of course not."

"You can catch a tape of the press conference

on the late news. I know you're a football fan. Anyway, will you have a drink with me after work? This is a sad day."

"Yes, sure. I'll meet you over there."

"Great. See you later."

She slowly replaced the receiver. Patrick had done it, she thought, her mind racing. He'd held his press conference and announced his retirement. Seth had said he'd been poised, but Seth could tell it had been very hard on Acer. Oh, Patrick. What a horrible thing to have gone through. All those reporters staring at him, waiting for him to go to pieces, then firing questions at him, and he . . .

Teddy? her mind echoed. Oh, for heaven's sake, it was a simple coincidence, that's all. Patrick happened to have a physical therapist named Teddy. For a fleeting, silly, heart-stopping moment, she'd thought he was referring to the enormous blue bear. Due to the fanciful path her mind had been taking since meeting Patrick Mullaney, she'd had the absurd notion that Patrick's reference to Teddy was somehow an indirect message linked to her! Good grief.

She was out of control. She really was. She was working much too hard, needed a vacation, was turning into a blithering idiot. If any of her friends knew the shape she was in, they'd have her shipped to the farm. She had to get a grip on herself concerning one Mr. Patrick "Acer" Mullaney.

"Lux?" Sharon said from the doorway, bringing her from her tangled thoughts.

"Yes?"

"You'll never guess what happened."

"Nothing would surprise me these days," Lux muttered.

"Pardon me?"

"Nothing," she said, forcing a smile. "What happened?"

"I was at the counter trying on one of the smallest caps and gowns on a little bunny when Mrs. Kingston came in."

"Oh, yes, she ordered the blue duck for her new nephew. It was ready to go."

"I know, but then she saw the cap and gown. Her youngest daughter is graduating from high school in May, and they're having a huge party for her. Mrs. Kingston ordered one hundred beavers, the school mascot, dressed in caps and gowns as favors. The school colors are yellow and green. She wants fifty of each."

"One hundred beavers?" Lux said, her eyes widening.

"Yes, the six-inch size. They're holding the party at one of the ritzy hotels, and she wants a beaver to be at each place setting. Cute, huh?"

"One hundred beavers," Lux repeated. "In caps and gowns. Green and yellow."

"Yep. Just think. We haven't even done the window display yet, or advertised the graduation gimmick. I was just standing there playing with one of the outfits and . . . bingo . . . we get an order like this. You'd better get on the phone to our suppliers, boss. What a genius you were to think of the caps and gowns. Oops, someone just came in." Sharon hurried away as she heard the sound of the bell over the door.

"One hundred beavers," Lux said, shaking her head. "In green and . . . Oh, mercy." What was going to happen when they actually advertised those screwy outfits? Well, chalk up one vacation, she thought, then reached for the receiver to the telephone.

Just after six o'clock, Lux stood outside the doors to Lulu Belle's and knew she didn't want to go in. The establishment was a replica of the Old West and was extremely popular with tourists. It was also the after-hours gathering place of many of the working people in Scottsdale, who converged en masse for drinks and conversation before heading home.

Lux often stopped in, enjoying the company of the friendly group. But today she wasn't in the mood. Nor was she in the mood to see Seth, whom she dated fairly regularly, and who was hinting that he'd like exclusive rights to her social hours. On their last date he'd been none too subtle about the fact that as an up-and-coming banker, it was time he gave serious thought to marrying and raising a family. Lux liked Seth, but she certainly didn't want to spend the rest of her life with him producing little bankers. No, she was definitely not in the mood to go inside. She just wanted to go home.

With a sigh, she pulled open the door and stepped in, waiting as her eyes adjusted to the semi-darkness.

"Lux!" Seth called. "Over here."

She made her way forward, seeing that Seth was with a group from the bank. Seth was good looking, she supposed, in a yuppie sort of way, and was pleasant company on a date, but she wished he'd drop his new program of wanting her all to himself. She just wasn't interested.

"Hi, honey," Seth said, patting the chair next to him.

Honey? Lux cringed, sitting down.

Seth kissed her on the temple. "How's my girl?"

How's my girl? Lux's mind repeated. Where was he getting this garbage?

"Hello, Seth," she said, then smiled at the others. "I can't stay long, just one quick drink."

"Your usual, sweetheart?" Seth said.

Sweetheart? Darn it, he was embarrassing her. "Yes, fine," she said.

"We're going to have a group toast to Acer Mullaney," Seth said, signaling to the waitress. "We're having a drink in his honor."

Patrick liked root beer, Lux thought. She should have ordered a root beer. Lord, she was getting hysterical.

For the next half an hour, Lux listened quietly as the group reminisced about fantastic plays that Acer had made in the past. There was, Lux realized, a sense of possessiveness in the fans, as though they had personally had a stake in Patrick's life, career, and the way he handled a football.

Oh, yeah? Lux thought smugly. She'd bet none of them had ever been kissed by Acer Mullaney with a six-foot blue teddy bear as a witness. Darn it, they spoke of Patrick as though he were a commodity, now labeling him damaged goods and useless to their cause.

They seemed, she admitted, genuinely sorry that Acer had been hurt, but were more concerned about who would replace him, and if they would get their money's worth at games during the next season. What about Acer, the man, the person? What about *him*? She'd had enough of this.

"I must go," Lux said, getting to her feet.

"I'll come by the shop tomorrow, Lux," one of the young women said. "I need a Warm Fuzzy for my little sister. She just had her tonsils out. Maybe I'll get one for myself, too. There are days after working in that bank that I'd like to hug a cute bear and feel better."

"Works every time," Lux said, smiling. " 'Bye, guys."

"I'll call you tomorrow, sweetheart," Seth said.

Okeydokey, snookums, Lux thought dryly. "Fine. Good night."

As Lux drove home in the van, she was not surprised that her thoughts were centered on Patrick. She wasn't thrilled about it, but she wasn't surprised. Now, she supposed, she'd do a rerun over dinner as Pete and Mick discussed Acer's press conference. Then, maybe, that would be that. She'd be able to, at last, close the final mental door on Patrick Mullaney.

At the house, Lux climbed through the window to find that Pete was the only one home.

"Mick took Sally to an early movie, then they were going for pizza," Pete said. "It's just you and me, kid. Want a sandwich?"

"Sure. Whatever," Lux said.

"Did you hear about Acer Mullaney?"

"I heard, I heard," Lux called over her shoulder, as she started down the hall.

As Lux and Pete ate a sandwich and fruit, he told her that a locksmith had actually shown up at the house.

"The guy said the lock is vintage World War Two or something. He's going to see if he can order a new one. What he had in stock wouldn't fit. If he can't find one, the whole door will have to be redrilled and shaped to accommodate a new lock. The back door is still stuck solid. I swear, Lux, when Mick and I painted the kitchen we never dreamed we were creating a burglar-proof back door."

Lux laughed. "We'll figure out a way to get it open. Don't worry about it." She paused. "It was nice of Mick to take Sally out."

"Methinks our Mick is smitten with our Sally. He talks about her and the baby all the time."

"Maybe he's just feeling protective, like a big brother. Sally's been here for months. Why would Mick suddenly have stronger feelings for her?"

"It just happens like that sometimes, I guess," Pete said, with a shrug. "One minute you're cruising through life, doing fine, then . . . whammo . . . someone gets to you and takes up residency in your brain."

Like Patrick. "That doesn't mean anything. Just because you think about a person a lot, it doesn't mean a thing."

"Ha!"

"Ha?" she said weakly.

"Ha. Mick thinks about Sally constantly. I'm telling you, Lux, Mick is bonkers for our little mama. Hey, no problem. I think she's a great kid. It's just that Mick would be taking on a helluva lot with Sally and a baby and, let's face it, he's busted broke. So am I, for that matter."

"Well, don't worry about it for now," Lux said. "One day at a time, Pete."

"Yeah, I suppose," he said, getting to his feet. "I've got to get ready to go."

"Pete?"

"Yeah?"

"Are you positive that it means something if you think about someone all the time?"

"Well, sure. That's one of the first signs of heart trouble. Guaranteed. Why?"

"Oh, I just wondered. Have you ever been in love?"

"I don't think so." He grinned. "I thought I was a couple of times, but I decided I wasn't in love, I was in lust."

"Peter!"

He shrugged. "What can I say? Well, I'm off to get ready for my date. You'll have the house all to yourself tonight for a change. You can put your feet up, sew your little buggers, and relax. Sound good?"

No. "Sure thing," she said, forcing a smile.

An hour later, Lux wandered through the living room, feeling restless and edgy. She'd cleaned up the kitchen, waved good-bye to Pete as he climbed out the window, and had gotten together her supplies to do her hand sewing. Two minutes after settling onto the sofa with a chipmunk that needed a smiling mouth, she was back up on her feet, pacing the floor.

And thinking about Patrick. And thinking about what Pete had said about people who constantly think about certain people. And, she fumed, driving herself crazy!

As the last of the gorgeous sunset disappeared, and darkness fell, Lux turned on the lights, sat down, got up, and paced some more.

She didn't want to hand sew one hundred beavers. She didn't want to deck the dumb, toothy creatures out in green and yellow graduation caps and gowns. She didn't want to put a silly grin on the chipmunk that was still on the sofa waiting for the rest of its face.

She wanted . . . She threw up her hands. . . . She didn't know what she wanted. She was in a strange mood, had never felt so charged with energy without being able to find an outlet for it. It was a distressing feeling, as though she were waiting for something. Weird. And disturbing. Very disturbing.

At the sound of a car pulling into the driveway, Lux practically dove onto the sofa and grabbed the chipmunk. She had no intention of explaining to any of her housemates why she had been pacing the floor rather than doing her sewing. Why any of them was home so early she didn't know, but she strived for a relaxed pose and a pleasant expression. She then proceeded to stick the chipmunk square in the nose with the needle.

"Oh, you poor baby," she said, then kissed the wound.

A knock sounded at the front door, and Lux jumped. Oh, for heaven's sake, she told herself, calm down.

She got to her feet, crossed the room to turn on the porch light, then pushed up the window and poked her head out.

"Yes? May I help . . . Patrick!" she said, her eyes widening. She was going to fall right out of the window in a dead faint, she thought wildly. Patrick Mullaney was there? On her front porch? In a white V-neck sweater with tawny curls peeking above the V, and faded jeans, leaning on his crutches, he was honest-to-goodness there? Really? Sherwood, snap out of it! "What a surprise," she said, wondering absently if her voice really sounded as wobbly as it had to her own ears.

"Hello, Lux," Patrick said quietly. "I know this is presumptuous on my part, and if you're busy, I'll understand."

"No, no, I'm not busy. The chipmunk will be grateful to you for life."

"The who?"

"Never mind."

"I'd like to talk to you, Lux. May I come in?"

"Certainly." She paused. "Oh, dear, maybe not."

"If I'm interrupting something . . ."

"No, you're not, honestly you're not. It's just that I'm not sure you should be climbing through windows with your bad knee."

Patrick came closer. "I beg your pardon?"

Lux's gaze swept over him and her heart began to race. "You drove your car?"

"Yeah, I can drive now. The Ace bandage is off my knee. It's time to start moving it, doing exercises, getting the muscles and ligaments back in shape. What did you say about the window?"

"The lock on the door is broken, and the back door is stuck closed with paint. Dumb, huh? The only way in is through this window. Maybe I should come out there."

Patrick smiled. Lux's heart did a somersault. "I think I can manage this," he said. "I hope nobody calls the cops."

"The thought has occurred to me that they might," Lux said. "Are you sure you should be doing this, Patrick?"

He came to the edge of the window. "Here, take my crutches."

"Well, all right."

Lux backed out of the window, then accepted the crutches in the next minute. She stood, hardly breathing, as one jean-clad, muscled leg came through the opening, another leg, then the bent-over remaining body of Patrick Mullaney. She stepped forward ready to give him the crutches, her hands on the grips.

Patrick's hands closed around hers as he lev-

eled himself up and towered above her. He kept
the majority of his weight on his good leg so as
not to crush her hands that were trapped beneath
his, but made no attempt to release her.

Lux slowly lifted her eyes to meet his gaze. They
were close, standing so close, she realized, and
she could feel his heat, smell his special, unique
male aroma, felt as though she were falling into
the depths of his beautiful brown eyes. Oh, she
was so glad to see him. So very glad that he was
there.

"Hello, Patrick Mullaney," she said, in a funny
little puff of air.

"Hello, Lux Sherwood," he said, his voice low
and rumbly.

Neither moved. Lux assumed she was breathing, but just to be safe, told herself to inhale, then
exhale. Her gaze never wavered from Patrick's.

"May I . . ." He cleared his throat. ". . . sit down?"

"What?" She blinked. "Oh, of course."

Patrick lifted his fingers to release her hands,
and she gestured toward the sofa. As he made his
way forward, she closed the window, then hurried
to remove the box, dumping the chipmunk uncer-
emoniously on its head.

"Would you like something to drink?" she said.
"I'm afraid I don't have any root beer, though."

Patrick placed his crutches on the floor as he
settled onto the sofa. "No, thanks."

Lux sat down a cushion away from him and
looked at him, waiting for him to speak again. He
was tired and it showed. He must have had a grue-
some day because of the press conference, and
now he was there, in her living room, sitting on
her sofa. She was so glad to see him, happier

than she wanted to admit even to herself, but why was he there?

"You said you wanted to talk to me?" she said, unable to bear the silence another second.

"Yeah, I did," he said, raking a restless hand through his sun-streaked hair.

"Okay."

"Did you see the press conference today?"

"Not yet. I was going to watch it on the late news. I heard about it, though. It was the main topic of everyone's conversation. It must have been very difficult for you, Patrick."

"It wasn't the high point of my life, believe me, but I survived."

"I heard that you have a private therapist to help you with your knee."

"No."

"No?"

"I have a gym in my house and a series of exercises to do. My injury is serious but not unusual enough to require special assistance. I have the self-discipline to do what I have to."

"But you told the reporters that you were working with . . ."

"Teddy," he interrupted. "Yeah, I know. That's what I wanted to talk to you about. I should have called you, Lux, thanked you for what you said to me that day at my house. I should have, but I didn't. I was hoping you might see the press conference, so I tried to tell you in my own way that I'd listened to you, that Teddy had gotten me through a very bad night and . . . Then I realized that I owed you more than that. I came here to thank you in person."

"Oh, Patrick, I didn't do anything. I was there, that's all. It could have been anyone."

He shook his head. "No, it was you. And Teddy. Lux, I . . . I quit fighting it all because of what you said. In the middle of the night, I grabbed that blue bear, and I . . ." He looked up at the ceiling for a long moment, then met her gaze again. ". . . I cried."

Instant tears misted Lux's eyes and she couldn't speak for a moment. "I'm glad," she finally whispered.

"It helped, it really did. Because of that night, because of you, and Teddy, I got through the press conference without falling apart. I tried to tell you by what I said to the reporters, but then I decided to come here myself. Besides, I wanted to see you again. You've been on my mind a lot, Lux."

"I've thought about you, too, Patrick," she said softly.

"Yeah?" he said, leaning toward her. He slipped one hand to the nape of her neck. "Come here, lovely Lux. I really would like to kiss you again. How do you feel about that?" His voice seemed to drop an octave lower. "Do you think my kissing you again is a good idea? Tell me, Lux, what do you think?"

Think? she repeated in her mind. Who could think at a moment like this? Okay, okay, she was thinking. And, oh, yes, she wanted Patrick to kiss her. And, oh, yes, he had a smooth delivery in that deep, sexy voice of his, lady killer that he was. But she was aware of his reputation, was alert, on guard. She was in control . . . sort of . . . so what harm was there in one little kiss?

"Lux?"

She moved next to him on the sofa. "I think it's a fantastic idea, Patrick."

"Glad to hear it," he said, then lowered his lips to hers.

Oh, yes, Patrick thought, then parted her lips and placed his tongue deep into her mouth. He needed this, he wanted this, he'd dreamed of this. Lux.

Lux slid her hands up Patrick's chest, relishing the feel of the lush material of his sweater and the steely muscles beneath. She circled his neck with her arms, and met his tongue with her own.

Patrick was there, her mind hummed. And it was glorious. He *had* been speaking to her at the press conference. Her! And he trusted her enough to tell her that he'd hugged his Warm Fuzzy Teddy and cried. Oh, Patrick. Oh, heavens, what was this man doing to her? She was so glad, so filled with joy that he'd come, that he was kissing her. She didn't want this kiss to end. Not ever.

Patrick's lips moved to her cheeks, her nose, her throat, his breathing rough in the quiet room. Then he claimed her mouth again in a searing kiss that brought a near-sob of pleasure from Lux. His hands slid to her back, bringing her closer, her breasts crushing his chest. She leaned into him, wanting more, taking more, giving more. The kiss went on and on.

Lord, how he wanted her, Patrick thought hazily. He ached with need, his arousal strong, heated, straining against the zipper of his jeans. Why Lux? She wasn't his type, he knew that. She didn't play the game, he knew that. She was different, special, rare and, damn it, he knew that. Then why in the hell did he want her more than any woman he'd ever met? Damn, *that* he didn't know.

Patrick tore his mouth from Lux's and took a deep, raspy breath. He gazed down at her kiss-swollen lips, the flush of desire on her cheeks, her lashes fanned on her lovely skin, then saw them slowly lift to reveal her blue eyes that were nearly smoky gray with passion. His heart thudded in his chest with a painful cadence.

"I think . . ." he said, drawing her arms away from his neck, ". . . that we'd better call a halt here."

"Why?" Lux asked, a dreamy quality to her voice.

"Lux, come on," he said gruffly.

"What?"

He set her away from him. "Yeah, you'd better snap out of it," he said, running a hand over the back of his neck. "And quit looking at me like that."

"Like what?" she asked, the last of the rosy glow disappearing.

"Are you kidding?" he said, his voice rising. "You look like a woman who has been thoroughly kissed and is asking for more. Well, guess what, lady? If I kiss you again, I won't stop. I'll take off your clothes and make love to you for hours."

"You certainly will not," Lux said indignantly. "You're taking a lot for granted here, Patrick Mullaney."

"Oh, yeah? Deny it, Lux. Go ahead, deny that you want me as much as I want you. No, don't bother. I know you want me."

"Well! You've got a great deal of nerve. Just who do you think you are?"

"The guy who was kissing you, damn it," he yelled. "The guy who felt you surrender in my arms. The guy who aches to bury himself deep inside you, and finish what we both . . . both . . . started here. That's who I am."

"Oh," she said weakly. "But I couldn't . . . I mean, I don't . . . That is . . ."

"I know," he said, his voice gentling. "I know you don't sleep around. I know I can't have you." He trailed his thumb over her cheek. "I shouldn't have kissed you, I guess, because I knew I'd want more. Ah, Lux, I've never known anyone like you. I've trusted you with very private things about myself, yet I have no doubts that my secrets are safe with you. I suppose it's all a matter of timing."

"Timing?"

"I've met you now when I'm in a bad place, a frightening place in my life. You're so different from the women I know. You've given me something they wouldn't even come close to understanding. Thing is, Lux, I don't have anything to give you in return."

His body, Lux thought. She'd settle for his body, in her bed, now, making love to her. Oh, who was she kidding? She couldn't do it, couldn't have a one-night stand. Yes, she wanted him. She wanted him with an aching intensity that was new, strange, exciting, and frightening. But she wouldn't know how to separate the physical from the emotional. She just wouldn't know how. Her heart would be involved in a joining with Patrick, and her heart would be broken.

Lux sighed. "I'm not worldly and sophisticated, Patrick, but you've already figured that out. I'm very honored that you trusted me with your secrets. I hope that things go well for you in the future and . . ."

"Hold it," he said, raising a hand. "Are you dusting me off here?"

She frowned. "I'm accepting in a mature manner the fact that you're dusting *me* off."

"I am not!" he said. Yes, he was. Of course, he was. Why would he hang around a woman who couldn't, wouldn't, satisfy his needs? He was going to climb back out that window and never see Lux again. Wasn't he? Damn right. He'd come there to thank her for what she'd done for him, for helping him through a rough time. But, damn it, she didn't have to be so calm, so understanding about the fact that he was walking out of her life.

"You're confusing me, Patrick," Lux said. "We both know I'm not a bed hopper, and you are. We both know that I don't have sex just because it would be a marvelous few hours, but you do. We both know—"

"That's enough," he roared. Lux jumped. "You're making me sound like a total sleazeball, a sex maniac."

"I certainly am not. I'm merely stating facts. You move in the fast lane, you—"

"Don't start your crummy list again," he said, folding his arms over his chest. "I've been insulted enough for one night."

"Darn it," she said, throwing up her hands, "what do you want from me?" Patrick smiled. "Don't answer that."

Patrick reached for one of her hands and held it. "Lux," he said, his expression now serious, "so much has happened to me lately that I can't sort it all out yet. All I know is that for some reason I can't handle the idea of crawling out that window and never seeing you again. Understand?"

"Yes," she said, nodding. Yes, she understood, because she felt the same way. But this was wrong. She and Patrick operated on different planes, in different worlds, with codes of conduct that weren't remotely close to matching up. If she was smart, she'd never see him again. If she was smart, she'd protect her heart from this man. And she had a sinking feeling in the pit of her stomach that she was about to be very, very dumb.

"What would you suggest we do?" Patrick said, stroking his thumb over her knuckles.

"Well," she started, then took a deep breath, "since it's quite apparent that we're not destined to be lovers . . ."

"Hell," Patrick muttered. Lux ignored him.

". . . and since neither of us is ready to accept not seeing each other again," she went on.

"Yes?" he said, leaning toward her.

"I guess . . ." She shrugged, then managed a very weak smile. ". . . we're going to be friends."

Four

Sweat poured off Patrick's glistening body as he sat on the edge of the padded table. A weighted leather band was strapped to his right ankle as he slowly lifted his leg, then lowered it again. The muscles in his leg, shoulders, and back bunched and moved beneath his slick, tanned skin as he gritted his teeth and repeated the process over and over. Up . . . Down . . . Up . . . Down . . .

"Friends," he said, his voice strained from the physical effort he was exerting. "That's what she said. It felt as though I'd been punched in the gut. Me, Acer Mullaney, friends, just friends, with Lux Sherwood? Hell, I want to make love to that woman!"

Up, then down. Again, then again, and again. "Anyway, before I could come up with something brilliant to say, a pizza box came through the window. I was so stunned by what Lux had said that I didn't even hear the window being opened, then in comes this pizza box. I nearly fell off the sofa. My leg is going to fall off. Thank God that's enough of these leg lifts."

Patrick unbuckled the weight, slid off the table, then limped across the room. He stepped into a swirling hot tub and sank down to his chin with a grateful sigh, not bothering to remove his sweat-soaked jogging shorts.

"Where was I?" he went on. "Oh, yeah, the pizza. Well, behind it was a good looking guy, who crawled through the window, then helped a very pregnant, pretty girl in. I was sure for a moment there that she was going to get stuck. Lux introduced them, and there was a hoopla because Acer Mullaney was in the house. But everyone calmed down and we shared the pizza. Ready for this? They live there, that Mick and Sally. They're not together. I mean, Mick isn't the baby's father, they each rent a room from Lux."

He reached over to adjust the temperature of the water, then settled back again.

"That doesn't make sense, because I asked Megan about Lux's business, Warm Fuzzies and Friends, and Megan said it's in an exclusive shop in Scottsdale. Not only that, but, according to an article Megan read, it's doing great. Why is Lux living in an ancient old house with busted locks, renting out rooms?"

He shook his head. "Then, to top it off, in through the window comes another guy: a tall, lanky number, who turned out to be Pete. He lives there, too! He and Mick play guitars and sing in a coffee house down near ASU while they're waiting for their big break into show biz. Unreal. They're nice people, all of them, but why in the hell are they living with Lux? And, man, oh, man, what am I going to do about a woman I ache for, who says we should be friends? Answer me that, buddy." He paused. "Nothing to say, Teddy? Well, hell."

The big, blue teddy bear just sat on the seat of an exercise bike and smiled.

Lux sat in her office at Warm Fuzzies and Friends and stared into space, a slight frown on her face.

Friends, she repeated in her mind for the umpteenth time. She and Patrick "Acer" Mullaney were going to be just friends. That was what she had told him last night just before Mick and Sally had arrived home. Friends. It had seemed like a good idea at the time, the only solution, but then why had she spent the night tossing and turning? Why had she, Patrick's friend, relived over and over those mind-boggling kisses they had shared, and felt desire thrum throughout her?

Well, she reasoned, that made sense. Her mind knew she couldn't make love, have casual sex, with Patrick. Her body, however, was a bit slow on the uptake and hadn't gotten the message yet.

She could handle this, Lux decided firmly. After all, having men as friends was nothing new to her. Mick and Pete were friends, were like brothers to her. *But friends with Patrick Mullaney?* That would mean no more kisses. That would mean not being held in those steely arms against that rock-hard chest. That would mean not fantasizing about what it would be like to make love with Patrick. Because, oh, yes, she had wanted him. Shame on her, but she had.

Well, no more of that stuff, she told herself. That delicious, wondrous stuff. No, sir. She and Patrick were just friends. Anything more than that was guaranteed heartbreak, and she didn't want her heart broken. She didn't want to cry when Patrick moved on to the next woman who caught his fancy. Friends was the answer, and friends it was going to be.

With a decisive nod and a lingering feeling of depression, Lux flipped open a file and began to check invoices.

Fortunately, the morning sped by. There were so many customers that Sharon had to call Lux up front to help, and sales were brisk. During momentary lulls, Lux replenished the shelves from the large storage area in the rear of the store. Many of the customers were winter visitors preparing to return home, and who were buying gifts for young relatives in the East.

Sharon began to pull the present display from the front window to prepare for the graduation push, and Lux cringed at the thought of the one hundred beavers already ordered. Even with Sally's help with the hand sewing, Lux realized, she couldn't keep up. She had to do something to ensure that all orders were completed on time.

"Sharon," she said quietly, as several people browsed in the store, "I'm thinking about hiring another salesclerk. The paperwork on my desk is piling up. I'm having trouble keeping up with the hand sewing, too, but I hate the idea of not being the one to finish each toy."

"Well," Sharon said, "I see your point, but you hate the paperwork, Lux. You're sentencing yourself to being cooped up in that office all day instead of out here with the people where you like to be. Why don't you hire someone who can handle the bookkeeping? You could deal with the customers, then do hand sewing in the slack times.

We could make that one end of the storage room into an office for a paper person."

Lux frowned. "Oh, well, I never thought of that. The coordinating of the orders for supplies, cutting, sewing, all of that, is so important. I always felt I should do it myself."

"It's your store, your business, built by hours and hours of hard work. You should be doing what you like best. You've earned that right. You don't see Iacocca putting on hubcaps."

Lux laughed. "There's hardly a comparison."

"Well, you get my drift," Sharon said. "I think you should . . . There's the bell. More people." Both women turned to look as the door opened. "Holy cow," Sharon whispered, "it's Acer Mullaney. Oh, Lux, he's gorgeous."

That, Lux mused, was putting it mildly. In jeans and a red knit shirt that accentuated his broad shoulders and bronzed skin, his hair tousled, Patrick was more than gorgeous. He was magnificent. He was also . . . *her friend.*

"Hello, Patrick," she said, smiling. Her heart was going nuts, totally nuts, beating like a bongo drum. Well, too bad, she was ignoring it. "How are you? I didn't expect to see . . . Where are your crutches?"

"I have a special brace on my knee for now," he said. "Hello," he said, looking at Sharon.

Lux made quick introductions as Sharon continued to stare wide-eyed at Patrick.

"Did you come for a Warm Fuzzy?" Lux said.

"No-o-o," he said slowly. "This is Warm Fuzzies and Friends, right? I came to take my friend— that's you, remember?—to lunch." He flashed her a dazzling smile. Sharon sighed.

"Oh, well, I . . ." Lux said. ". . . I . . . It's awfully busy here today and . . ."

"Oh, go, go," Sharon said. "It's letting up some. I can handle it."

"Great," Patrick said. "All set, Lux?"

Yes? No? her mind raced. Patrick hadn't invited her to lunch, he'd announced they were going without even consulting her. That was rude. Well, it wasn't totally rotten rude, it was medium rude. And she did have to eat.

"Lux?" Patrick said.

"I'll get my purse."

Patrick had a low-slung, royal blue sports car with a white interior. They were the colors of the Blue Falcons football team, but Lux didn't comment. Patrick seemed to have little difficulty driving, since his injured leg was needed only to press on the gas pedal.

Lux watched him from beneath her lashes as he smoothly shifted gears, his large, tanned hand covering the knob of the gearshift in the center panel. She could see the muscles of his thighs move beneath the soft denim of his jeans, and she swallowed heavily.

"Well!" she said, a trifle too loudly. "What have you been doing with yourself all morning?"

Talking Teddy's ear off, Patrick thought, hiding a smile. "Working out, doing my exercises that the therapist set up for me."

"Was it painful?"

He shrugged. "No pain, no gain."

"I suppose."

"I like your store," he said. "It's really homey and inviting. You seem to be doing a lot of business, too."

Lux sighed. "Yes, we are. I have to make some decisions as to how to handle it all."

Patrick pulled into a parking lot and turned off the ignition. "Trader Vic's suit you?"

"It's one of my favorite places," she said, smiling over at him.

It was also very dark inside, Patrick thought, getting out of the car. There was little chance of anyone recognizing him in the dimly lit restaurant. He didn't feel like sharing his time with Lux with anyone. His *friend* Lux. Hell. He was definitely going to have a problem with this friends-only program. He should just walk away from her and forget the whole damn thing. But he wasn't going to, he knew it, and for the life of him he wasn't sure why.

They were seated in a cozy alcove with high-backed rattan chairs, and placed their orders for seafood platters.

"Now then," Patrick said, "go back to what you were saying. Business is booming, and you have decisions to make. Like what?"

"It's rather boring, Patrick."

"Not if it's about you. Go ahead, lay it on me."

"Well, okay," Lux said. "You see . . ."

Lux outlined the problems she was facing at Warm Fuzzies and Friends, stopping only when the waitress put their plates in front of them. Patrick listened intently, nodding several times as he began to eat. Lux took a bite of shrimp, then looked at him.

"That's it," she said.

"It sounds to me that Sharon is right. You should hire someone to do the paperwork so that you can do what you want to. That's privilege of rank."

"Yes, but that paperwork is vitally important.

Any slipup could cause major delays. I have a reputation to protect."

"Then screen your applicants very carefully," Patrick said. "In the meantime, I could help you out."

"What?"

"I was an accounting major in college, Lux. I'm a whiz at numbers, details, your ever-famous paperwork. It's my thing, as they say."

"Oh, but I . . ."

"Look, I'd like to go back to my house this afternoon and do another series of hours of exercises for my knee. I'd feel as if I were giving it my all, but I can't do that. The therapist was clear on the subject. If I overdue my workouts I'll cause more damage than good. I have to be patient, stay on the schedule he gave me. I'm facing some long, dull afternoons. You'd be doing me a favor by giving me a project, and I'd be helping you in the process. Think about it, Lux. What are friends for, if not to give each other a hand?"

Friends? Lux thought. Who? Oh, yes! She and Patrick were friends. But, oh, goodness, it was hard to remember that when the candlelight was flickering over his rugged, tanned features, when he was gazing at her with his gorgeous eyes, when . . . Halt, Sherwood!

"What do you think?" Patrick said, then took a bite of a flaky roll.

"Accounting major?"

"Yep. Top of my class," he said. She certainly was beautiful in the candlelight. Her hair was so dark and shiny, swinging free around her face. Her eyes were big, and blue, and bright. And her lips. Oh, man, those lips were begging to be kissed. By him. Only by him. Hold it, Mullaney. Those were *not* damnable friendly thoughts. "I'm very good," he said. "At paperwork," he added quickly.

And kissing, and holding, touching, and . . .

"I'm sure you are," she said, hearing the thread of breathlessness in her voice. "But you're a celebrity, a very famous person. I can't quite see you in a little office in the back of a store that sells stuffed toys."

"It will suit me just fine," he said, his voice low.

"Oh," Lux said weakly.

Their gaze held. Sensuality weaved around them, creating crackling awareness of the one, the only one, within their view. Senses were heightened; seeing, smelling unique, familiar feminine and masculine aromas. A yearning to feel, caress, to taste. Need and want were nearly palpable entities in the highly charged air. Hearts raced. Heat gathered low and heavy in bodies awash with desire. There were no sounds around them, no low murmur of voices, clashes of dishes, bursts of laughter across the room. There was only Lux and Patrick, and the echo of their own heartbeats rushing in their ears.

"How's everything here?" the waitress said.

"Oh, good Lord," Lux said, jumping in her chair. She covered her heart with her hand.

"We're fine . . ." Patrick said, then cleared his throat. ". . . fine."

"Okay," the woman said, then moved away.

Lux looked at Patrick, her eyes wide, the color suddenly draining from her face. Dear heaven, her mind raced, what had just happened between them? It was frightening, strange, and . . .

"Lux," Patrick said, his voice slightly husky, "I—"

"Excuse me," she said, getting to her feet. "I'm going to the powder room."

Patrick watched as Lux hurried away, then released a long breath, only then realizing he'd been hardly breathing. He slouched back in his chair, and ran his hand down his face.

That, he decided, had been weird. Very weird. It was as though the world had stopped, and he and Lux had gotten off, stepped into a hazy twilight zone that had contained only the two of them; nothing else, no one else, just them.

And it had felt so damn good!

There had been a rightness about that strange, timeless moment, a feeling of everything having fallen into its proper place when, in actuality, his life was in total chaos. Separate and apart from the churning heat of desire within him, had been a warmth like nothing he'd ever felt before. Damn it, what was Lux Sherwood doing to him?

Patrick drained his glass of root beer, and scowled.

In the ladies' room, Lux splashed water on her face, then patted her skin with a paper towel. Then and only then did she have the courage to glance at her reflection in the mirror.

She looked the same, she thought with relief. Same face with its familiar eyes, nose, mouth; regulation equipment for a face. But she didn't feel the same. Something had happened in the eerie second? minute? hour? that she'd been pinned in place, seeing only Patrick.

Yes, it had been frightening but . . . but there had also been a soothing warm fuzzy feeling intermixed with what she knew had been desire.

Oh, mercy, she didn't know how to handle all of this.

So? she asked her reflection. Now what? She couldn't hide in the bathroom for three days until Patrick got the message that she wasn't coming out. She had to march back to that table and . . . Do what? Say what?

"Lawsy, Mr. Mullaney," she drawled to her image in the mirror, "did y'all notice that little ol' strange spell that fell over us? What do y'all think that was, sugar plum?" She frowned. "Lux, shut up."

She picked up her purse, stomped to the door, and yanked it open. When in doubt, she told herself, fake it.

Lux returned to the table, settled into her chair, and forced a smile onto her lips. "So, Patrick," she said, "you're really serious about doing some paperwork at Warm Fuzzies and Friends?"

Hell, no, he thought. Forget that nonsense. He was putting distance between himself and Ms. Sherwood. Whatever was happening between them was beyond his scope of understanding, and he didn't want any part of it. No, sir. No way.

"Yes," he heard himself say.

"I see," Lux said, fiddling with her napkin. "Well, all right, I guess we could give it a try. Tomorrow is Sunday, and we're closed on Sundays. How does Monday sound? You could come in the afternoon after you've done your exercises for your knee. I'll pay you, of course. I'm sure we can settle on a fair wage and—"

"Lux . . ."

"I won't hold you to any promise or anything. I mean, if you find the work as dull as dishwater just speak right up and say so. It's very tedious and—"

"Lux . . ."

She plunked her elbow on the table and rested her forehead in her hand.

"Don't speak to me," she said, her voice trembling. "Don't say one word."

"Hey," he said, jiggling her arm, "don't fall part on me here. I'm shook up enough as it is."

Lux slowly lifted her head. "You are?"

"Damn right," he said gruffly. "Whatever that was that happened between us, Lux, was very weird. I've never experienced anything like that before, and I have no idea what it was."

She straightened in her chair. "Oh. Really? Well, goodness, that makes me feel immensely better."

"It does? Why?"

"Because you're very worldly, experienced, you . . ."

"Are you going to start clicking off one of your lousy lists again?" he said, glowering at her.

"No, no," she said quickly. "All I'm saying is, if someone like you doesn't know what that was, then how could someone like me possibly know? Therefore," she went on, pointing a finger in the air, "we'll just chalk it up to one of those quirky things that happens every so often that there's never any real explanation for. Okay?" She smiled brightly.

He wanted to kiss her, Patrick thought suddenly. He wanted to haul her across that table into his arms, and kiss her until neither of them could breathe. She was talking too fast, her eyes were as big as saucers . . . She was scared to death. He wanted to hold her, comfort her, tell her that everything was all right. He wanted to protect her. And he wanted to make love to her.

"Okay, Patrick? We'll just forget it?"

"Okay," he said gently.

"Good. You're a very nice . . . friend. I really must be getting back. Thank you for the lunch."

Patrick nodded, then signaled to the waitress. Friend, he repeated in his mind. He was really starting to hate that word.

Neither spoke during the drive back to Lux's store.

"No parking places," Lux said, glancing around. "That's all right, just drop me off. Thank you again for lunch, Patrick. I'll see you on Monday afternoon."

"Lux, I . . . Yeah, okay, I'll be here."

Lux hurried onto the sidewalk, then waved as Patrick drove away. Oh, God, she thought frantically, what had she done? She had to have been out of her mind to agree to have Patrick work at the store. She didn't want him there. Yes, she did. No, she did not! Well, maybe she did.

"Oh, cripe," she said, then spun around and went inside.

Sharon was busy with a customer, and Lux hurried into her office and sank onto her chair behind the desk.

She was not, Lux told herself firmly, going to give one moment's thought to what had happened in the restaurant. That eerie, sensuous, tingling spell that came over them made it seem as though they were the only two people on the face of the earth. It was not worth dwelling on. It was, as she'd said, just one of those strange, unexplainable things that happened to people every once in a while.

"But not to me," she said aloud. "It's never

happened to me before. Oh, forget it. Right now, Sherwood. Forget it."

She reached for an invoice and stared at it for a full five minutes before she realized that it was upside down.

"I'm telling you, Teddy," Patrick said, as he pedaled the stationary exercise bike, "it was weird. I told you what happened in the restaurant, how everything just faded out except Lux. Oh, she is something. And she's driving me crazy. Why, I ask you, did I say I'd work down there in the afternoons? Starting tomorrow I trek to Warm Fuzzies and Friends to see your relatives, and do Lux's paperwork. Dumb, huh?"

He adjusted the pressure of the bike, then checked the mileage gauge. Sweat glistened on his body as he resumed a steady pedaling rhythm.

"I can do the work, of course," he went on. "I haven't seen her system, but that stuff is right up my alley." He shrugged. "What the hell, it will give me something to do in the afternoons for a while, and it will help Lux out. She looked tired when we had lunch yesterday. This is no big deal. So I see her for a few hours every day? So what? We're just friends."

He frowned and increased his speed. "Just between you and me, buddy, that dream I had about Lux last night would not qualify for activities befitting friends. What is that woman who is not even my type doing to me? Maybe this is good, Teddy. You know, seeing her every day will make me realize that she momentarily knocked me over, but I'll get things back in their proper perspective. Yeah, that makes sense. Sure glad you're here to talk things over with, pal."

The big, blue bear sat against the wall with a towel slung around his neck, and smiled.

Lux sewed on Sunday until her fingers ached, then baked a cake, did her wash, vacuumed, dusted, then pulled everything back out of the kitchen cupboards and made another cake.

Sally and Mick had disappeared through the window in midmorning, then Pete had announced that he was going to go play guitar with a bunch of guys who were getting together in the park.

The house was empty and quiet, stretching Lux's frazzled nerves to the limit. She was restless, edgy, hadn't slept well, and she was angry. Angry at herself, for try as she may, she couldn't push the thought, the image of Patrick Mullaney from her mind. Not sewing, or cleaning, or baking, had helped divert her attention from Patrick.

Lux flopped onto the sofa in a dejected heap, and stared at the ceiling. Tomorrow, she mused. Tomorrow afternoon Patrick would come to Warm Fuzzies and Friends to start helping with the paperwork.

Hooray! He was coming tomorrow.

No, no, wrong reaction. She didn't want him there. Unless . . . Yes, of course! What better way to get Patrick into his proper slot in her head than to be with him every day as friends? Talk, work together, laugh, share, as friends. It would all fall into place, she'd come down out of the clouds, face the reality that he was a ladies' man, and she'd get on with her life. Without Patrick "Acer" Mullaney haunting her waking hours and creeping into her dreams at night. Splendid.

"Very good," she said, bouncing to her feet. "Excellent, in fact. I amaze myself sometimes."

With a smile firmly in place, she went into the kitchen where, for the lack of anything better to do, she baked another cake.

Five

Lux studied her reflection in the full-length mirror in her bedroom the next morning and decided that she looked very attractive, professional, and in control. Her gray suit with the pale blue blouse that had a soft bow at the neck even made her appear, she was convinced, older and more mature. As long as no one saw her hike her skirt up around her thighs to crawl out the window, she'd be all set.

She'd brushed her hair until it shone, and watched in the mirror as it fell back into place when she turned her head. Yes, she gave the impression one should have when one was in charge of one's own business.

Lux sank onto the edge of the bed and sighed. What a hoopla she was making over what she was wearing, she thought dismally. She'd had a frantic notion that if she *looked* in control, she might *feel* in control . . . of her life. But she didn't feel in control, she knew it, and also knew the source of her inner turmoil. Patrick Mullaney.

Patrick. He was there, with her, constantly in her thoughts. He floated through her dreams at night, and greeted her upon awakening in the morning. Every stern lecture she gave herself regarding the fact that Patrick was the wrong man for her had not diminished his haunting presence.

She knew he was a ladies' man, a man of no commitments or promises. He lived for the moment and moved in the fast lane. That he was even stepping into Lux's world was a fluke, brought on by his injury. He was marking time, waiting to return to high living, and the women who came with that life-style.

Patrick "Acer" Mullaney was not the man to fill that niggling void that Lux had discovered in her existence. Oh, yes, she mused, she now knew what that feeling was. It was the inner yearning to love and be loved in return by the man of her heart. That confusing restlessness, sense of searching for something, had become crystal clear. She was whole within herself, a complete woman with goals and dreams. She knew who she was, and was proud of her accomplishments. She was ready, it was time to love.

And every time she thought of that unknown man who might be her partner in life, up popped Patrick Mullaney in the front of her mind.

But Patrick was the wrong man!

"Darn him," she said, getting to her feet. He was consuming her brain, the rotten person. She should be viewing someone like Seth with new insight, seeing him as perhaps a part of her future. Seth? Oh, ugh, not Seth. She couldn't imagine spending the rest of her life with a man who got all charged up over the going prime rate. Okay, not Seth. But not Patrick, either. Patrick didn't believe in futures. He had a revolving door on his bedroom. The rotten, rotten person.

Lux climbed through the window with less-than-ladylike gracefulness, and drove toward Scottsdale.

All right, she told herself, as she maneuvered through the heavy traffic. She had all the facts now. While she was not scrambling to find a special man, she was receptive to the idea, and certainly wouldn't run in the opposite direction should he appear. She also knew that she'd never see him under the present circumstances, because the image of Patrick would be blocking her view.

Seeing Patrick every afternoon at Warm Fuzzies and Friends would work to her benefit. Her mission was clear: She would get Patrick out of her system by overexposure. It would work. It had to.

"Friends," she said aloud. "Patrick and I are only friends." The time he spent at the store would give her proof positive of that. It just had to. Because of it didn't, Patrick "Acer" Mullaney was going to break her heart. That rotten, rotten, rotten person.

Lux and Sharon spent the morning waiting on customers, and completing the graduation display in the window. Sharon chattered on about her husband of six months, and told Lux that while Acer Mullaney was a gorgeous hunk of stuff, she'd leave him in Lux's capable hands.

At noon, Lux went out for a quick sandwich, and when she returned Sharon took her lunch hour. The store was momentarily empty of customers, and Lux glanced around, being greeted in all directions by the smiling faces of the perky stuffed toys.

"We did it, Gran," she said softly. "Just as we said since I was a little girl. Thank you, Granny, so very much."

The bell over the door tinkled, pulling Lux from her thoughts. Patrick entered. He was dressed in black slacks and a yellow dress shirt open at the neck. Lux stared at him, felt the increased tempo of her heart, the curling heat deep inside her, and fought the urge to turn and run.

This man, she now knew, was a threat to her future, her peace of mind, her hope of finding a lasting relationship.

"Hello, Patrick," she said, praying her voice was steady.

He walked slowly forward, limping slightly, no readable expression on his face. He stopped in front of her, the counter separating them. Their eyes met and held.

Beautiful, Patrick thought. She is just so beautiful. He wanted to kiss her, hold her, and . . . No, dammit, where was his good sense? There was a purpose to his being there that did not include hauling Lux Sherwood into his arms and kissing the living daylights out of her. He was supposed to be getting her off his mind so he could get back to the life-style he knew and enjoyed with the women who understood how the game was played. But, oh, Lux was beautiful.

"How did your exercises go this morning?" Lux said, switching her gaze to a lavender goose.

"Fine," Patrick said, shoving his hands into his pockets. "The knee is responding well to the therapy. I was lucky, really. I'll come out of this okay. I just know that if I play football I'd run the risk of never walking properly again. The knee couldn't come back another time. I've accepted that now."

"Have you decided what you want to do?"

He shrugged. "Offers are pouring in, and my agent is looking them over. My knee is top priority, then I'll decide. In the meantime, here I am ready to dive into your paperwork. Lead me to it, boss." He smiled at her.

Lux matched his expression. "Well, I can't leave the front until Sharon gets back. There is a stack of folders on my desk you could look through, though. It might give you an idea of my system. I'll join you as soon as Sharon returns."

"Okay."

"My office is right around the corner there. Patrick, if you don't like the work, you will tell me, won't you? You didn't promise anything. You have no commitment to me. I mean, to Warm Fuzzies and Friends," she added quickly.

His smile faded. "Don't I?" he said, his voice low as he looked directly at her.

"No," she said, hardly above a whisper. "There is . . . no commitment."

"We'll see, Lux."

The bell over the door jangled, and Lux jumped in surprise. Patrick looked at her for another long moment, then limped away. Lux forced a smile onto her lips and greeted the customer.

In Lux's office, Patrick sank onto the chair and absently rubbed his throbbing knee.

No commitment, he repeated in his mind. They'd been talking about the store, the paperwork he'd agreed to do, but yet . . . There had been hidden messages there, innuendos of something more, deeper, personal. No commitment. What had Lux been saying, really saying? That she intended to follow through on her stand that they were just friends? That she wanted no part of him as a man to her woman? That he wasn't supposed to kiss her, hold her, want to make love to her?

"Well, hell," he said aloud. No, now wait a minute. If that *had* been the message she'd been delivering it suited his purpose just fine. Right? Right. She wasn't his type.

She was Lux.

Special, rare, beautiful Lux.

Lux with the outer veneer of the successful businesswoman, and the underlying essence of innocence and vulnerability. Lux, who evoked feelings of protectiveness in him and, yes, possessiveness. Beautiful Lux, with her shiny, swinging hair, expressive eyes, and lips that beckoned to be kissed.

Lux, Patrick thought, who was weaving silken threads around his heart, and creating a warmth within him like nothing he'd ever known.

No commitment? he asked himself again. Just friends? Someone he'd walk away from without a backward glance once his knee was healed, and he'd chosen a new career? No. No, he didn't like the sound of that at all. And he didn't like the knot that twisted in his gut at the thought of it.

Well, now, Patrick thought, this was interesting.

He laced his hands behind his head, leaned back, and stared at the ceiling.

Very, very interesting, he mused. And confusing, and rather unsettling. His life was undergoing major changes. He was closing the door on a career he'd had for years, and he'd accepted that the night he'd hugged poor old Teddy and cried. Could it be that he was ready for other changes, too? Was it possible that he wanted more than the fast-lane life-style with its string of faceless women? Was his preoccupation with Lux a message from his heart?

Patrick leaned forward and crossed his arms on the desk, a frown on his face. Why didn't he know? he wondered. Hell, it was all happening too fast, that's why. He'd met Lux just when he'd found out his football days were over, and it had all jumbled together. He had to sort this through, figure out exactly what it was that he was feeling toward Lux.

No commitment?

Maybe, maybe not. But he sure as hell was going to find out. The program was changed, the signals had to be reread. He wasn't automatically going to work on getting her out of his system, he was going to discover exactly what place she had in his new life. He'd watch, listen, really pay attention to Lux *and* to himself.

"And talk it all over with Teddy, of course," he said, with a chuckle.

Still smiling, Patrick reached for a file, flipped it open and began to read.

A half hour later, Sharon bounced in the door.

"Is he here?" she said, in a loud whisper.

"Yes," Lux said, smiling. "He's in my office."

"Oh, be still, my heart," Sharon said, flattening her hand on her breast.

Lux laughed. "You're a married woman, remember?"

"I know, and I love my David. But, Lux, it's the law of the land. Men like Acer Mullaney, Tom Selleck, all those delicious specimens were meant to be looked at, drooled over, gawked at from afar." She paused. "Well, some of us can't touch, but then again, others of us can."

"Oh?"

"Don't play dumb with me, Lux Sherwood. I've seen the way Acer looks at you. Oh, those eyes of his. They remind me of a fawn's."

"Chocolate chips, fudge sauce, and . . . Forget it," Lux said, fiddling with a bow on a bear.

"Ah! I knew you couldn't be immune to his attributes. You'd have to be dead. So, what are you going to do about it?"

"Do?"

"Do."

"Nothing. Sharon, for heaven's sake, Acer Mullaney is a ladies' man. He has more women than I have Warm Fuzzy Bears."

"People change. He could change if he met the right woman."

"I'm not having this conversation with you, Sharon. I'm going to go see how Patrick . . . Acer is doing."

"You do that. Take your time." Sharon said, smiling brightly.

Lux glared at her, then left the front of the store and walked to her office door. She stopped, her eyes wide as she looked in the room. Papers were piled everywhere; on the desk, chair, filing cabinet, the floor.

"Patrick?" she said, aware but not caring that her voice had squeaked.

He glanced up and smiled at her. "Hi."

She walked slowly forward, stepping over a neat row of papers. "What are you doing?"

"Figuring out your system."

"And?"

"Okay, here it is. You're spending too much time shuffling papers. You place an order for, say, twenty toys of various sizes, then mark them off by date when they come in."

"Yes. So?"

"So, it's easy to see how your suppliers work. They do a batch of six-inch animals, then send them to you. Later, the twelve- or twenty-inch, or whatever arrive. You have to go back through the original orders to check them in."

"Right."

"Wrong. It's wasting time. If you wrote the original order on separate sheets according to the size of the toy, you could file away a lot of papers early on and never have to touch them again. You'd know at a glance what hadn't arrived yet, and be able to check them off in flash when they got here. Get it?"

Lux nodded slowly. "Yes. Yes, I do."

"I thought I'd transfer all these orders to the new system."

"That would be a lot of work, Patrick."

He shrugged. "That's what I'm here for," he said. Among other things. Also on the agenda was to find out exactly what that beautiful whisper of a woman standing across the room meant to him.

"I could help you, Patrick. All this bending and standing has got to be hard on your knee."

Oh, sweet bliss, Patrick thought, he couldn't have customed-ordered a better setup. "I'm trying . . ." He sighed dramatically. ". . . to ignore the pain, be macho, you know what I mean?" He sighed again for good measure. "Life must go on. I'll get those papers back up off the floor." He paused. "Somehow."

"Oh, my goodness, no," Lux said anxiously. "You mustn't do that. That would be like exercising your knee, Patrick, and you know what you said about not doing more than the therapist prescribed for one day. You just sit back down in that chair, and I'll bring these papers to you when you're ready for them."

"You're such a kind person, Lux," he said, turning to hide his smile. "I hardly know what to say."

Lux narrowed her eyes as Patrick hobbled to the chair and sank into it with yet another sigh.

Was he smiling? she wondered. Was that, or was that not, a very smug little smile tugging at his lips? No, it couldn't be. A man in pain didn't smile. And yet . . .

"Ready?" Patrick said, all innocence.

"What? Oh, yes, of course."

"Very good," he said, picking up a file. "We'll start with the orders for the material used to make Teddy's relatives."

Lux laughed. "How is Teddy?"

"Superb. He keeps me company while I do my exercises every morning. Maria has finally decided not to do him any more bodily harm. I knew Teddy would win her over in time. The guy has charisma. Yep, Teddy is top-notch, first-class."

And so was Patrick Mullaney, Lux thought. There he sat, talking about a big, blue, furry teddy bear as though it were one of his best friends. Oh, yes, she did like this man. She respected him, too, for the way he'd pulled himself together and accepted the end of his football career. There was depth to Patrick Mullaney, so much below the surface of the outer façade of the high-living, swinging playboy.

Teddy bears and root beer—Darn him, it wasn't fair, Lux decided. Those, combined with Patrick's masculine magnetism, his incredible dark eyes, were going to put her in an early grave.

Or break her heart.

"Lux?"

"Who? Oh. Yes. What papers did you say you wanted first?"

Patrick chuckled. Lux narrowed her eyes suspiciously again. They got to work.

Several hours later, Patrick pulled another sheet of paper out of the typewriter, scanned it, then smacked it into an open file on the desk.

He was dying, he fumed. He was a dying man. He hadn't counted on Lux's feminine presence filling the small room to overflowing. He hadn't counted on her fragrance assaulting his senses, or the coiled heat that churned low in his body when she leaned over his shoulder, her silky hair brushing his cheek. He hadn't counted on being aware of every move she made . . . every luscious move . . . or on their fingers touching with the force of an electric jolt as she gave him the papers. *He was dying!*

And Lux? he mentally rambled on. She was as cool as a cucumber, strictly business. Yes, he'd been very impressed with the way she knew, from memory, practically every little detail of the inner workings of Warm Fuzzies and Friends. But, damn it, he might as well have been a statue sitting in that chair for all the personal attention she *hadn't* paid to him. Hell.

Patrick glanced at Lux out of the corner of his eye and saw her replace a file in the cabinet. He ought to grab her and kiss her senseless, he decided. He'd pull her onto his lap, nestle her soft curves to his hard body, cover her mouth with his. That would make her remember that he was in the room. Wouldn't it?

He shifted in his chair as his body responded to

the mental image of Lux cradled on his lap eagerly returning his kiss.

Or would she pop him in the chops? he wondered. Damn it, was she really serious about this "friends" garbage? Didn't Lux Sherwood feel anything for him at all? Didn't she remember the fantastic kisses they shared, the eerie, warm, wonderful spell that had fallen over them when they'd been together? Yes, by damn, she'd responded to his kiss, he'd felt her give way to her desire. And she'd been as shook up as he had when that rosy spell had trapped them. Ms. Sherwood was not as cool and in control as she would have him believe.

Well, now he felt better. He'd nearly panicked there for a minute thinking that Lux didn't care about him at all. She did care . . . at least a little.

Patrick ran his hand over the back of his neck and shook his head. He sounded, he admitted, like a kid with his first crush. He was Acer "Love 'em and Leave 'em" Mullaney, and he was being turned inside out by one woman.

By Lux.

And it felt so damn good.

Patrick's gaze swept over Lux again and he smiled. His feelings for her, he knew, were growing stronger. They were new emotions, things he'd never experienced before, and he wasn't going to fight them, not a bit. Whatever this was he was registering for Lux was filling him with warmth, a tremendous sense of peace and well-being.

Was he falling in love with Lux Sherwood?

He didn't know, Patrick realized. Maybe he wouldn't recognize love if it hit him with a brick. What he *did* know was that he had every intention of finding out just exactly what all these new emotions meant, and he'd discover the depths of

Lux's feelings for him in the process. He hoped. She was getting very adept at treating him like a damnable friend.

"Quitting time," Sharon sang out, poking her head in the door. "My, my, what a mess. Must be a sign of genius. I'm off to cook dinner for David. 'Bye, Lux. 'Bye, Acer."

"Good-bye," they said unison. Sharon disappeared.

"Well, the afternoon certainly flew by, didn't it?" Lux said brightly, not looking at Patrick.

"We must have been having fun," he said gruffly.

"Ready to go? I'll lock up."

"Lux, I forgot to mention that I've solved the problem of your stuck back door. I'll follow you home."

Lux looked at him quickly. "You're going to follow me home? Now?"

"Yeah. I should have told you, but it slipped my mind. You'd like your back door fixed, wouldn't you?"

"Yes, of course, but what are you going to do to it?"

"Trust me," he said, getting to his feet.

Trust him? Lux thought, following him out of the office. With her back door, yes. With her heart, never. How she'd survived the afternoon cooped up in that little room with Patrick, she'd never know. He'd looked so good, and smelled so good, and she'd wanted him to kiss her so much she'd nearly crawled across the top of the desk to get to him. The only thing that had kept her from making a complete fool of herself was Patrick's businesslike attitude. She'd been, as far as he was concerned, invisible. What a blow to her feminine ego. No, darn it, that was how friends behaved.

"See you at your house," Patrick said, out on the sidewalk. He limped away.

Lux watched him for a long moment. With a sigh, she headed for her van.

At the house, Lux drove into the driveway, and a moment later Patrick pulled in after her. As she slipped off the seat, a huge, white Lincoln parked at the curb.

"There he is," Patrick said, as he leveled himself out of the sports car.

"He who?" Lux said, walking to the rear of the van. "Oh, my gosh, that's the biggest man I've ever seen in my life. Who is that?"

"Hammer Henderson. He's a tackle for the Blue Falcons."

"Hey, man," Hammer called, striding toward them, "is this the place that needs my brawn?"

"This is it," Patrick said. The men executed a high-five greeting, then Patrick made introductions.

"Hello," Lux said, tilting her head back to look up at Hammer.

"Ma'am," he said. "I understand you have a door that could use a little muscle power."

"Oh, good heavens," Lux said, her hands flying to her cheeks, "you'll kill it."

Patrick and Hammer laughed. Lux was convinced that the ground had trembled.

"Naw, I'll treat it right," Hammer said, grinning. "Acer, you look good. How's the knee?"

"Coming along."

"Damn, we're going to miss you next year, man. It just won't be the same without you. I don't blame you, though, for pulling out. I wouldn't risk crippling myself up, either. Have you decided what you want to do?"

"Not yet."

Hammer looked at Lux, then back at Patrick. "Checking things out, huh?"

Patrick smiled. "Something like that."

" 'Bout time, Acer. Yep, you're due. Say, Lux, you should see Acer with my baby girl. What a pair. Mullaney here is great with kids, really great."

"Cork it, Hammer," Patrick said, laughing. "Let's go operate on the door."

The window on the porch flew open and Mick crawled out, followed by Pete. They vaulted over the railing on the porch and joined the trio.

"Hammer Henderson," Mick said. "I'll be damned." Patrick made introductions again.

"He came to fix the back door," Lux said, but no one paid any attention to her. The four men were engaged in a loud conversation centered on football, and outstanding plays made by Acer and Hammer. "I still say he's going to kill the poor door," Lux said to a painted rabbit on the side of the van.

The men started toward the back of the house, still talking football. Lux shrugged and followed.

Patrick liked children? she mused, her glance sliding over his delectable rear view. Hammer certainly had made a sales pitch on the subject. Why had he done that? Oh, who could understand men?

At the back door, Hammer ran his enormous hands around the frame, then nodded.

"No sweat," he said.

"We tried everything," Mick said. "That paint is like concrete."

Hammer leaned his shoulder against the center

of the door, braced one leg and one hand on the wood, then shifted his weight. The door popped open.

"Oh!" Lux gasped.

"I told you he wouldn't kill it," Patrick said, grinning at her.

"Piece of cake," Hammer said. "You guys need to chip off the dried paint before you close it again."

"You bet," Mick said. "Lord, Acer, it's a miracle you're alive, considering you had about six guys like this blitz you that day they creamed your knee."

"Tell me about it," Patrick said, smiling.

Hammer frowned. "I'd give anything to call that play back. We screwed it up so damn bad. Those animals were past us and onto Acer before we came off the line. I heard his knee go. I'll never forget that sound."

Lux shivered and looked at Patrick.

"Give it a rest, Hammer," Patrick said quietly. "It wasn't your fault. We've been all through that. What's done is done."

Hammer shook his head. "It shouldn't have happened." He paused. "Well, your door is fixed, and my wife and daughter are waiting for me. Nice meeting you all. Lux, have Acer bring you by the house. I'd like you to meet my family."

"Thank you, Hammer," Lux said, "and thank you for fixing the door."

"No problem. See you soon, Acer. Don't forget, bring Lux to visit."

"Yeah, I will. See ya," Patrick said, as Hammer walked away.

"Let's get this dry paint off, Pete," Mick said. "You're staying for dinner, aren't you, Acer? It's

Lux's turn to cook. She's got something that smells great brewing in the crockpot."

"It's just stew," Lux said. "I doubt that Patrick would—"

"I'd be delighted," Patrick said. "Could you show me where to wash up, Lux?"

"Oh, well, yes, of course," she said, then hurried into the house.

Patrick, Mick, and Pete shared very male, very knowing smiles, then Patrick went into the house.

"You can wash up in that bathroom," Lux said, pointing off the kitchen. "I'll go change my clothes."

"Take your time," Patrick said pleasantly. "I'll just make myself right at home."

Lux beat a hasty retreat without looking at him, his low, sexy chuckle following her out of the kitchen. In her room, she changed into jeans and a red T-shirt, brushed her hair, sank onto the edge of the bed, and wondered frantically if she was having a nervous breakdown.

She couldn't handle this, she thought, pressing her hand to her forehead. After all those hours in her office with Patrick, she simply couldn't handle sitting across the table from him while he ate her stew. It was too much for one day, it really was.

"Oh, Lux, would you just shut up?" she said, then stomped out of the room.

She found Patrick in the living room talking to Sally, who had eased herself onto a straightback chair.

"Hi, Lux," Sally said.

"Hi. Sally, do you feel all right? You're awfully pale."

"I'm okay, just tired. I've had a roaring backache all day."

"Stay put," Patrick said. "I'll help Lux get dinner on."

"No," Lux said quickly. "I mean, you should rest your knee, Patrick."

"My knee is fine. I'll set the table."

"Oh, why not?" Lux said, throwing up her hands in defeat.

"Is something wrong, Lux?" Patrick asked, all innocence.

"No," she said, starting toward the kitchen.

"That's good," he said, following close on her heels. "The stew smells delicious."

"Stew is stew," she said, entering the kitchen. She turned to look at him. "Thank you for having Hammer come by to fix the door. That was very thoughtful of you."

"I'm a very nice person," he said, grinning at her.

Yes, he was, Lux thought. He really was. "Hammer feels very badly about what happened to your knee, doesn't he?"

"Yeah. The play got fouled up, that's all. It happens sometimes, and it's not one person's fault. I've told him that. Where's the stuff to set the table?"

"In that first drawer. I'll make a salad."

"Done," Mick said, striding into the room. Pete followed him. "The door is as good as new. That Hammer is something."

Patrick chuckled. "He's big, all right. I was always glad he was on my team."

"He has a wife and daughter?" Mick said. "It's hard to picture a huge guy like that with a little baby. I mean, I've watched him play for years, looking like he eats raw meat, and creams quarterbacks for the pure joy of it, and it turns out he's . . . I don't know."

"Just a man, an ordinary man," Patrick said. "Most of us are, Mick. Oh, there are some hot dogs in the league, and some classic space case dumb jocks. But on the whole, we're just guys earning a living like anyone else. The press has a tendency to paint us in a different light." He looked at Lux. "About a lot of things. I've had my share of women, and I admit that. But a lot of the stories were publicity stuff, favors done for an actress or model trying to get her picture in the paper. The Blue Falcons cooperate with that junk. It goes with the turf."

"Interesting," Mick said.

"And true," Patrick said. "Like I said, I've had my share, but not to the extent that the papers would have you believe."

"More's the pity," Pete said with a laugh. "Come on, Mickey, let's wash for dinner."

Lux turned back to the counter and began to tear lettuce into a bowl. Patrick came up next to her and ran his thumb over her cheek.

"Were you listening to what I said?" he asked quietly.

"Yes."

"But did you hear, really hear it? Look at me, Lux."

She turned her head slowly to meet his gaze.

"I'm no monk," he said. "I like women, they've always seemed to like me. But, Lux? I'm not as racy as the papers have made me out to be. I've never cared before what they printed about me, but now I do, because it's important to me that you believe me. I've never intentionally hurt anyone. I never would." His gaze slid to her slightly parted lips. "Never."

Then he gathered her close to his body and

claimed her mouth with his. Lux leaned into him, savoring his heat, and strength, and aroma.

She'd been waiting all afternoon for this. So many hours.

Patrick lifted his head. "Think about what I said. Okay? I'm being as honest with you as I can." He stepped back. "I'll set the table."

Lux nodded, unable to speak as she drew a wobbly breath. She turned back to the counter and stared into the salad bowl.

Oh, Patrick, she thought, she didn't know what to believe. For all she knew this was Ladies' Man Mullaney's standard procedure for seduction, his well-practiced program of lowering a woman's resistance. She just didn't know! She was so confused and frightened. She should tell Patrick not to come back to Warm Fuzzies and Friends the next day. Tell him to go, leave her alone, just please, please, disappear from her life.

But as that thought flitted through her mind, Lux dismissed it.

She didn't have the inner strength to tell Patrick to go away.

It was too late.

And if she fell in love with Patrick Mullaney and he broke her heart, if she cried, she'd have no one to blame but herself.

Six

As dinner began, Lux felt as though she were split in half, functioning as two separate people.

Mick and Pete seemed determined to center the conversation on football, the Blue Falcons, and Acer's career in particular.

Patrick, on the other hand, strove to steer the chatter to more general topics, continually trying to draw Lux's opinion from her and include her in the discussion.

A part of Lux was aware of Patrick's efforts, and she chalked up more points in his favor on what was now a scorecard in her mind. That list was growing longer and stronger, tallying increasing numbers of attributes that showed Patrick to be dear, sweet, thoughtful, charming. . . .

But another part of Lux remained confused and frightened, unable to decipher fact from fiction. Patrick's reputation as a ladies' man haunted her, as did her own lack of experience. The realization was chilling that she was unable to determine if

Patrick was sincere or merely traveling on his well-rehearsed road to seduction.

In between those two extremes, was Lux the woman, responding on a physical, desire-laden level to Patrick Mullaney, the man. His mere touch, glance, or smile caused a fluttering heat deep within her, a blush on her cheeks, an increased cadence of her heartbeat. The need, the want, to be held in Patrick's arms, to feel his mouth on hers as he fitted her to his aroused body, hovered close in Lux's jumbled mind. The sexual scenario went further; seeing her becoming one with Patrick, making love, giving and receiving all that they were to each other.

She couldn't go on like this, Lux thought dismally. She was falling apart. What a fraud she was! Independent businesswoman Lux Sherwood was, on the surface, an intelligent, ambitious, successful person. Underneath she was a quivering lump with the sudden, urgent need to grab a Warm Fuzzy bear and hug it for comfort.

Somehow, she vowed, she had to determine who and what Patrick "Acer" Mullaney was.

As Patrick, Mick, and Pete refilled their plates with stew and salad, Lux glanced at Sally, only then realizing that the young girl hadn't taken more than one or two bites of her dinner. Sally appeared even more pale and drawn than she had earlier, and kept one hand resting protectively on her protruding stomach.

"Sally," Lux said, interrupting Pete's dissertation on potential quarterbacks for the Blue Falcons, "are you all right?"

Pete stopped speaking. All eyes were riveted on Sally.

"Sally?" Mick said. "Say something."

"I . . . Um . . ." she started, then swallowed heavily. ". . . I think the baby is coming."

Mick lunged to his feet, knocking his chair over in the process, the color draining from his face. "No, it's not. It's not time yet. Tell it, Sally. Do something."

"Mickey, sit down," Lux said sternly.

"No, dammit," he yelled.

Patrick reached over, put Mick's chair back in place, then grabbed Mickey's shirt and plunked him in the chair.

"Sit," Patrick said.

"But—"

"Shut up," Patrick said. "Give the poor girl a chance to answer our questions." He paused and looked at Lux. "What are we supposed to ask her at a time like this?"

"Oh, for heaven's sake," Lux said. "Sally, are you having pains regularly?"

"About every six or seven minutes," she said.

"Oh, good Lord," Mick said, leaping to his feet again. Patrick hauled him back onto the chair.

"My back ached all day," Sally went on, "then just before dinner I had this really sharp pain, and now they keep coming closer and closer together." Her eyes filled with tears. "Oh, I'm so scared."

"*Now* you get up," Patrick said, releasing his hold on the back of Mick's shirt.

Mick hurried around the table, dropped to one knee beside Sally, and wrapped his arm around her shoulders.

"It's okay," he said. "It's not your fault the kid doesn't have a calendar in there. Everything is going to be fine. I'll be right there with you every minute, Sally."

"Until he passes out on his face," Pete muttered. "He's white as a ghost."

"Oh!" Sally gasped, clutching her stomach.

"Oh," Patrick echoed, flattening his hand on his own stomach. "That looked like it hurt. We can't just sit here. Don't you people have a game plan for this?"

"Yep," Pete said, getting to his feet. "I call the doc, Lux gets Sally's suitcase. Mick phones the club and says we won't be in. We had alternate setups depending on who was home. This is Plan A. Mick, go call the club. We're doing Plan A. I'll get the doc's number. Mickey!"

"Forget him," Patrick said. "He's gone. Pete, you make both calls. Cars?"

"I'll drive," Pete said.

"Lux and I will follow you in my car."

"Got it," Pete said, striding from the room.

"Oh," Sally moaned.

Patrick cringed. "That kid is practicing to be a punter."

"I'll get her suitcase," Lux said, getting to her feet. "Patrick, you don't have to go to the hospital. I mean, after all, you were invited for stew, not—"

"I'm going," he said. "Mick, help Sally up and out to the car. At least she can go through the back door instead of crawling out the window. Mick?"

"Huh?"

"He's totally wasted," Patrick said, getting to his feet. He went around the table and gently assisted Sally to her feet. "Okay?"

"Yes," she said, managing a weak smile.

Patrick reached down, grabbed the back of Mick's shirt again, and dragged him up.

"Mick," Patrick said, "say something encouraging to Sally. Damn it, man, open your mouth or I'm going to deck you."

"Wonderful," Lux said and started toward the kitchen door.

"I love you, Sally," Mick said. "I swear I do. I love you and this baby."

"Oh, Mickey," Sally said.

Patrick nodded. "Not bad. That was very nice."

Lux stopped and turned. "He loves her? Huh?"

"Don't you start that," Patrick said. "Go do your thing for Plan A."

"Oh, yes, of course," Lux said, hurrying out of the room.

Somehow, the jangled group managed to start toward the hospital. Patrick followed close behind Pete's car. Lux clutched her hands tightly in her lap.

"The baby is early," she said, "but not enough to be concerned about." She paused. "I don't think. What do I know? Sally is young, healthy, everything will be fine. Won't it? Sure it will. Mickey loves Sally. Pete was convinced that Mick felt that way about her, but Mick actually said he loved her and the baby. Pete said that Mick doesn't care about the baby's father. That's so sweet. Oh, ignore me, Patrick, I'm babbling. But I'm just so nervous."

He glanced over at her and smiled. "We all are, I guess. One little baby sure can push a lot of people's buttons."

"It's awfully nice of you to come along."

"There's nowhere else I want to be, Lux," he said, his voice low. "What's happening tonight is important to you, and I want to share it with you. It's as simple as that."

Or as complicated as that, Lux thought. Why?

Why did he want to share it with her? Why did . . . Oh, she just couldn't think about all that now.

"Lux, let me ask you something. It's none of my business, but . . . Well, from what I've seen, you're very successful at Warm Fuzzies and Friends. Why do you rent rooms? It's hard to believe you need the money."

"I don't need it. I don't charge that much rent, either. We divide up the chores, maintain the house. Pete and Mick painted the kitchen instead of paying rent one month."

"And stuck the door closed."

"True. It was their first attempt at painting. Except for the door, they did a nice job."

"Where did you find those three? I guess I really don't understand why they're there."

"After my grandmother died, I packed up a lot of her things to donate to a charity thrift shop. Pete and Mick were working part-time driving the truck. They came to the house to pick up the things. We chatted, and they said they were struggling musicians really living hand to mouth. I don't know, Patrick, there I was in that big old house with all that room, and they needed a place to live."

"And Sally?"

"She came into Warm Fuzzies and Friends looking for a job six months ago. I said I wasn't hiring at the moment, and she burst into tears. She was at the end of her rope, so alone, frightened, been deserted by a heartless man when he found out she was pregnant. I brought her home with me."

"Because she needed you," he said quietly.

"Well . . . yes."

"I see," he said. And he really did. He could still

hear the trembling in Lux's voice when she'd been in his house and talked about her parents. He could still hear so clearly her words, "They just didn't need me." It was coming together like pieces of a puzzle. Lux needed, desperately, to be needed. But did she have room in her life to be loved? Oh, he was sure that Sally, Mick, and Pete loved her, but he was talking about a different kind of love. Man and woman. Woman and man.

Lux and Patrick?

He didn't know yet, wasn't sure if he was falling in love with her, but if he did grow to love her, was there a place in her life for that kind of commitment and relationship? Or was the void that had been left by her parents filled by the needs of Sally, Mick, and Pete? Was that enough?

There were so many questions. And he intended to find the answers to every one of them.

At the hospital, Sally was whisked away while Lux filled out the necessary papers for admittance. Everything was in order, and the group was directed to the maternity floor waiting room.

"Now what?" Mick said, raking a hand through his hair.

"We wait," Lux said.

"How long?" Mick said.

"There's no way to know, Mickey," she said.

"I want to see her," he said. "No, I don't. I can't stand it when she's hurting like that. I'd end up yelling at her stomach, telling the baby to knock it off, and get the hell out of there."

Pete chuckled. Patrick nodded as though there were some logical reasoning behind Mick's statement. Lux rolled her eyes.

Patrick sank onto a leather sofa. "I've never had a baby before. When Hammer's daughter was born, he came pounding on my door in the middle of the night to tell me it was a girl. I've never been on the scene like this."

"And you were there," Pete said, in a dramatically rumbly voice. "I should have been a TV announcer. You've spent your share of time in hospitals, Acer."

"Yeah, but all I got out of it was a glued-together knee. Sally has a little tiny person inside of her. That's really something when you stop to think about it. She's walking around with a miracle."

Quick tears misted Lux's eyes. Oh, Patrick, she thought. Oh, darn him. He was doing his sweet and wonderful number again. If she went no further in her mind than the man he was at moments like these, it would be so easy, so very easy, to fall in love with him. But the doubts were there, too.

"I want to marry Sally," Mick said. "That baby will be ours."

Lux went to Mick and hugged him. "You'll be a fantastic husband and father, Mickey."

"I've got to make plans, figure out how to—"

"Let's just get this baby here first, okay?" Lux interrupted, smiling. "One step at a time."

"Speaking of time," Mick said, "how much longer is this going to take?"

"We just got here, man," Pete said. "Relax. You can't rush these baby people. Right, Acer?"

"Right," he said, then shrugged. "Hell, I don't know," he said, under his breath.

Lux sat down in a chair.

"Look at it like this," Patrick said. "It's good practice for the future, Pete. Mick is coming unglued here, but when we have a kid we'll be pros at this."

"Count me out," Pete said. "I have places to go, people to see. Marriage and babies are not in the cards."

Patrick spread his arms out along the top of the sofa and stared up at the ceiling. "A lot of guys say that. A lot of guys change their minds." He shifted his gaze very slowly to Lux, no readable expression on his face. "Happens all the time."

Now what was he saying? Lux thought, her heart racing. Oh, trying to figure this man out was impossible.

An attractive blond nurse stepped into the room.

"News?" Mick said. "You have news about Sally?"

"Sorry, Dad," she said, smiling. "I'm just trying to find one of the doctors who isn't answering his page." She glanced around the room. "Acer! My word, what are you doing here?"

He grinned at her. "Having a baby."

"You? Not a chance. You'll never stand still long enough to get caught in the diaper trap. That poor jangled soul over there is obviously the daddy-to-be. How's the knee?"

"Good."

"Glad to hear it. You're back in action, huh? Well, maybe not on the football field, but in all the places where it really counts. Give me a call. It's been ages since we had some fun together. Gotta run."

"See ya, Brenda." Patrick glanced around and saw three sets of eyes riveted on him. "That was Brenda," he said lamely. "She's a nurse. I would have made introductions, but I can't remember her last name."

Pete laughed. "Dig yourself in a little deeper, Mullaney. You can't remember her last name?"

Patrick looked quickly at Lux, then shifted uncomfortably on the sofa. "Well, no, because I haven't seen her in a long time. A very long time. Ages and ages. Years."

Pete hooted with laughter. Lux rolled her eyes again. Mick began to pace the floor. Lux then met Patrick's gaze, and he shrugged helplessly, smiling at her. It was an endearing smile, a little-boy-caught-in-the-cookie-jar smile.

"Years and years," Patrick said. He patted the cushion next to him on the sofa. "Come here."

Lux laughed softly and went to sit next to him. "You're a rogue, Patrick Mullaney," she said, still smiling.

His eyes widened. "A rogue? Now, that is a classy word." She smelled good. He liked her close like this, next to him. "Do you think Mick is going to survive this?" he whispered in her ear, as he circled her shoulders with his arm.

Who? Lux thought. *Oh, Mickey, yes, of course.* There was such heat radiating from Patrick's massive body. Heat that was weaving its way in and around her, causing her pulse to skitter. Oh, how safe and protected she felt in the circle of Patrick's arm, tucked close to his side, relishing his strength. What a delicious warm fuzzy feeling.

"Sally is the one with the work to do," she said, knowing her voice wasn't quite steady. "But once she holds that baby, I know she'll feel it was all worth it."

"And you, Lux?" he asked. "Do you like babies?"

She looked up at Patrick, and he was just inches away. Her heart did a crazy little tap dance.

"Yes," she said, hardly above a whisper. "Yes, I'd like to be a mother someday."

"You'd be a terrific mother," he said, his warm breath fluttering over her lips.

Her bones were dissolving, Lux thought. She was going to turn into a rag doll and slither right off that sofa into a heap on the floor. She wanted Patrick to kiss her, now, right there in front of Mick and Peter, and maybe Brenda What's-her-name. She wanted him to make it clear that she was his, and he was hers, they were . . . they were what? An item? Lovers? She was the current woman in Patrick's long string of willing women? Darn.

What was happening to her program of being just friends? she asked herself. It was shot to smithereens, that's what. She'd crossed over an invisible line, and now wanted more, so much more, from Patrick Mullaney.

Was this love?

Was she slowly but surely falling in love with Patrick "Acer" Mullaney?

If she was, Lux knew, there would be nothing she could do to stop it. She hadn't had the inner fortitude to send him away, and she'd have no control over her heart and the direction it might take her. If only she weren't so confused, so torn between what was fact and what was fiction. If only she knew what Patrick felt, really felt, for her. Time, she supposed, would supply the answers.

And in the meantime? she wondered. Patrick was a virile, healthy man. Each kiss they shared spoke of his rising passion, his desire to go further, to make love with her. Could she do it? Could she become one with this man, not knowing what the future held for them? Oh, why did everything have to be so complicated? Why couldn't she just live for the moment? Why did she have to think in terms of love, commitment, forever and ever? She was an old-fashioned prude.

"Hey," Patrick said, sliding his hand slowly up and down her arm, "where are you? Why the frown?"

"What? Oh, I was just thinking."

"What's taking so long?" Mick said.

"Cripe," Pete said, then slouched onto a chair. "You're driving me nuts."

"Well, hell," Mick said, then resumed his pacing.

Patrick kissed Lux lightly on the temple. "I'll be right back," he said. He got to his feet and limped out of the room.

"He's a good man, Lux," Pete said.

"He's a ladies' man, Pete," she said quietly.

"Maybe he was, but you heard him say that guys change their minds about things."

She shifted to face him. "But how would I know that? How do I know what's true?"

"You'll know," Mick said, stopping in front of her. "Believe me, Lux, you'll just know. You have to trust yourself a bit here, and trust Acer."

"Trust him? Based on what? He has a reputation of—"

"Yeah, yeah, I know," Mick said, raising his hand to silence her. "But there's something about the way he looks at you, the things he says, that tells me he cares. I nearly scared myself to death when I realized I was in love with Sally. But, dammit, Lux, what if I'd run from what I knew was true? I'd have lost her, and that little baby that is going to be as much mine as it is hers. I don't want to see you get hurt by Acer, but I don't want you to miss out on something special, either."

"Amen to that," Pete said, nodding. "Sometimes, I think, you have to take a chance, run the risks. Are you in love with Acer, Lux?"

"I don't know," she said, throwing up her hands.

"I've never felt like this about anyone before, but I don't know if it's love."

"Don't worry about that part," Mick said. "If you fall in love with him, you'll know."

"How?"

Mick shrugged. "It's hard to explain. It's just suddenly as clear as a bell. Give it some time."

"I don't like being so muddled up," Lux said.

"Tell me about it," Mick said, laughing. "I have to figure out how to support a wife and baby. But I'll do it, somehow. Having Sally, loving Sally, knowing she loves me, will be worth whatever I have to do."

"Ain't love somethin'?" Pete said with a grin. "I hope to hell it isn't catching. First Mick, then Sally, now Lux."

"I said I didn't know if—" Lux started.

"Who's kidding who here?" Pete interrupted. "You should see your face, your eyes, when Acer walks into the room. You're a goner, Lux Sherwood, I don't care what you say. As for Acer? I repeat, he's a good man. There, I've said my spiel. The rest is up to you."

"Oh, thanks," Lux said, glaring at him.

Patrick came back into the room, and Lux looked at him, then back at Pete.

Pete smiled at her. "A goner," he repeated. "That fact, darlin', you can take all the way to the bank."

Lux glowered at him again.

Patrick tore the cellophane from a deck of cards. "Gin rummy anyone? A penny a point."

"You're on, Mullaney," Lux said, rubbing her hands together.

Patrick narrowed his eyes. "Do I detect a bit of overenthusiasm here?"

"Get your wallet ready, Acer," Pete said, getting

to his feet. "We have all learned the hard way that Lux's grandmother taught her more than just how to make stuffed toys. Gin rummy? Oh, you poor fool. Well, at least it's not poker. She'd really clean out your clock."

"I'll be damned," Patrick said, grinning.

Lux got up and walked to the table in the corner. She settled into a chair, folded her hands primly on the top of the table, and smiled.

"Gentlemen," she said, "ante up."

At midnight, Lux had a mound of pennies in front of her and a smug smile on her face. Patrick plunked the cards in the middle of the table.

"I quit," he said. He leaned toward her. "Do you cheat?"

"There's no need to, sir. I happen to be a superb player. Would you care for a game of twenty-one?"

"Not on your life, Diamond Jim," Patrick said. "Besides, we've hit on every nurse and doctor on the floor to exchange nickels and dimes for pennies. You've got them all. Are you sure you don't cheat?"

"Don't be rude," she said, beginning to stack her pennies. "Aren't you a gracious loser?"

"No!" Patrick said, slouching back in his chair.

Mick got to his feet. "I'm going to go check on Sally again. I can't take much more of this." He left the room.

"I imagine Sally has about had it too," Pete said. "They keep telling Mick that everything is fine, but it sure is slow."

"Don't ask me," Patrick said. "I don't know anything about this stuff."

Mick came barreling back into the room. "She

just went into the delivery room. I saw her. She waved at me, smiled too. Oh, man, this is it."

Patrick started to get up, then sat down again, clutching his knee.

"Patrick?" Lux said anxiously.

"It's okay. It just stiffened up while I was sitting here losing my life's savings. Have you no heart, woman? I'm an unemployed beat-up jock. I have a six-foot blue bear to support."

"Tsk, tsk," Lux said.

"Are you people deaf?" Mick yelled. "Sally's having the baby right this second."

"Mickey, hush," Lux said, "or they'll throw us out of here. They'll tell you the moment there's news. That nurse promised you she'd come and find you. Calm down."

"What are you going to name the baby, Mick?" Patrick asked.

"I don't know," he said, shrugging. "We never talked about it."

"Poor kid," Pete said. "It'll go through life answering to 'Hey, you.'"

Fifteen minutes later a nurse in her fifties appeared in the doorway. Everyone was instantly on their feet.

"Yes?" Mick said. "Yes? Yes?"

The nurse smiled. "A beautiful baby girl. Six pounds, five ounces, with a dab of blond hair, and a healthy cry. Congratulations."

"Oh . . . my . . . God," Mick said.

Then to everyone's wide-eyed amazement, Mickey passed out cold on the floor.

It was almost two hours later before the weary group entered the back door of the house.

"Oh, ugh," Lux said. "Everything is still sitting on the table from dinner."

"Leave it," Pete said. "It can't be much worse than that in another few hours. Come on, big daddy," he said to Mick. "I'm pouring you in the sack. And, yes, Mickey, Elizabeth Lux is the most beautiful baby I've ever seen. Okay? Have we finally covered that for tonight?"

"She *is* the most . . ." Mick started.

"We know, we know," Pete said, grabbing his arm. " 'Night, all," he called, as he hauled Mick out of the kitchen.

"Elizabeth Lux," Lux said wistfully. "She really is . . ."

". . . beautiful," Patrick finished for her. "Yeah, she's cute. Kind of red and wrinkled, but she's got a great set of lungs."

"I'm so honored that Sally named her after me."

"She wanted to do it. She owes you a great deal."

Lux looked up at him quickly. "No, she doesn't, Patrick. She doesn't owe me a thing. If anything, I'm the one who is grateful for . . . never mind."

Ah, Lux, Patrick thought. He understood exactly what she was saying. Lux was grateful to Sally because Lux had felt needed all those months. Couldn't Lux see that? Maybe not. Maybe she didn't understand her own deep, inner pain caused by her parents.

"I'd better get out of here and let you get some sleep," he said.

"I need to unwind first. Would you like a piece of cake? We have a large supply of cake at the moment."

He shrugged. "Sure, if you're having some."

"Just push those dishes aside. Milk? Coffee?"

"Milk sounds good."

Lux brought the dessert to the table and sat opposite Patrick. There was a stillness in the house, a gentle silence that suddenly seemed to wrap itself around them like a cocoon.

There was not, Lux told herself firmly, anything intimate about eating cake and drinking a glass of milk in the company of a man. Unless, of course, that man happened to be Patrick Mullaney.

"Good cake," he said. "Did you make it?"

"Yes."

"I guess Mick and Sally will be moving out soon. You know, looking for a place of their own."

"Well, there's no rush. Elizabeth Lux will sleep most of the time at first. She won't disturb us. Mick has to figure out how to make more money."

"I realize that, but I also think they'd like to have their own place to start their lives together as a family." He paused. "They have each other now. That's all they . . . need."

Lux frowned. "What are you trying to say, Patrick? If there's some kind of message here, I'm too tired to get it. Did I miss something?"

He looked at her for a long moment. "No," he said, shaking his head. "Forget it. We're both tired. I'll hit the road."

"Yes, you should get off that knee. Don't worry about coming to the store tomorrow if you're weary. Sleep late, then do your exercises in the afternoon. You probably were on your knee far too long today and . . ."

"Damn it, Lux," Patrick said, smacking the table with his hand. Lux jumped. "I'm not one of your causes, I don't *need* you hovering over me like a mother hen."

"Well, excuse me," she said, starting to rise.

Patrick trapped her hand on the top of the table with his, forcing her to sit back down. He leaned toward her, a muscle jerking in his jaw.

"My *needs*," he said, stressing the word, "run in a different direction. I *need* to kiss you, hold you, touch you. I *need* to make love to you until we're both too exhausted to move. I'm sick to death of being your damn friend. And I sure as hell won't fill the gap that's going to be left when Mick and Sally move out."

"I . . . I don't understand what you mean. I understood some of it, but . . ."

"Did you get the part about my wanting to make love to you?" he said, his dark eyes flashing. "Did you?"

"Yes," she whispered.

"There's something happening between us, Lux, that is not, definitely not, friendship in its purest form. Pete and Mick are your friends. I don't fall into that category. Yes, lovers can be friends, too, but you and I are not on the plane that you, Mick, and Pete are. Understand?"

She nodded, her eyes wide.

"Dammit, don't you dare sit there looking frightened of me. What do you think I'm going to do? Throw you on the floor and ravish your body? All I'm saying is we deserve a chance to find out what this thing is that's happening to both of us. Forget the friends crap because I've had it with that. And, by damn, don't think for one minute that I'm going to be the next on your list of needy souls."

"Needy souls? What are you talking about?"

Patrick slouched back in his chair and stared up at the ceiling for a long moment. He sighed, a weary-sounding sigh, then looked at her again.

"Never mind," he said quietly. "My timing is so bad it's a sin. We're too tired for this. It's too heavy, too deep. Lux, just concentrate on the first part for a minute, okay? Do you agree that there's something happening between us that's not laid-back friendship?"

Lux ran her tongue nervously over her bottom lip before she spoke. "Yes."

"Don't you want to know what it is?" he asked, his tone gentle.

"I'm not sure."

"Do you honestly think we have any choice?"

"I . . . No, I guess not. I tell myself that I should . . . But then I . . . Oh, Patrick, I don't know."

"Give us a chance, Lux." He got to his feet and came around the table, limping badly. He pulled her up into his arms. "Don't you want the answers to what this is?" he said, close to her lips. "Don't you?" He slid his tongue over her bottom lip. "Don't you, Lux?" he trailed a ribbon of kisses down her throat. "Lux?"

She trembled in his arms. "Yes."

"We'll take it slow and easy. I won't rush you. Everything will be fine, you'll see."

"Patrick, I—"

"Shh," he said.

And then he kissed her.

He kissed her softly, gently, and sensuously, and Lux was so very tired and confused that tears filled her eyes and a sob caught in her throat. She was frightened by the things that Patrick had said that she didn't understand, and equally fearful of those she'd understood. She was torn between the urge to cling to him and never let go, and the one to run as fast and as far from him as she could.

Patrick lifted his head and cradled her face in his hands. "Good night, Lux. I'll see you tomorrow."

She could only nod, and didn't move as he stepped away, then left the house, closing the door quietly behind him. It was several more minutes before she had the strength to put one foot in front of the other and go to her bedroom.

At his house, Patrick hobbled down the hall to the gym and turned on the lights. The pain in his knee was white hot, and he went into the bathroom and swallowed two aspirin. He gritted his teeth as he crossed the room to the hot tub and adjusted the dials. After stripping off his clothes and the brace on his knee, he lowered himself into the soothing, warm water, stretching his arms along the rim and sighing deeply. His gaze fell on the blue bear.

"I really screwed up tonight, Teddy," he said. "I tried to make Lux see what's going on inside of her, make her realize her need to be needed is out of control. But my timing stunk. I'm an idiot."

He shook his head. "I pulled it out, though. Sort of. I put the heavy duty stuff on a shelf, got her to agree to drop this 'just friends' junk, and give us—the woman, the man, together—a chance. Yeah, I accomplished that at least. Lord, my knee is on fire. I overdid it today, but I really did want to go to the hospital with Lux. You should see Elizabeth Lux, Teddy. She looks weird, but I like her. I stared at her and thought about being a father, having a little baby, and a wife, of course."

He shifted his leg and cringed as the pain radiated all the way up his back. "Teddy, I sorted through everything as I was driving home. As tired as I am, as much as my knee hurts, I still managed to put the pieces together, find some of the answers."

He reached behind him to increase the temperature of the water, then looked at the bear again. "So, here it is, buddy, bottom line." He took a deep breath and let it out slowly. "I, Patrick 'Acer' Mullaney, am in love with Lux Sherwood."

Teddy kept right on smiling.

Seven

Patrick slept in late the next morning, and when he awoke, he was relieved to find that his knee was no worse for wear from the previous day and night. He called Warm Fuzzies and Friends to say he would be in around two after completing his exercises. Sharon informed him that Lux had also called and wasn't coming in until noon. Sharon chattered on about the exciting arrival of Elizabeth Lux, then said she'd see Acer later.

Patrick showered, ate breakfast, then headed for the gym. Teddy, Patrick decided, should wear more than a bow and a towel around his neck, and tugged and pulled a Blue Falcon football jersey onto the furry toy. Teddy now wore Acer Mullaney's number sixteen, and Patrick told him he was a dashing athletic figure.

"Want a job?" Patrick said. "They need a quarterback, you know. This jock has called it quits."

Patrick strapped the weighted belt onto his ankle and began the painful leg lifts, his body soon glistening with perspiration.

Unreal, he mused, continuing the steady rhythm and ignoring the pain. When he'd first met Lux he'd been shaking in his shorts about his future. He'd been angry, frustrated, entertaining flashes of self-pity because he'd been robbed of his career in one bone-crushing moment. He hadn't wanted to accept the truth that his playing days were over, and felt that someone should pay, blame should be placed. It had all been churning within him like a festering sore, waiting to explode.

And then Lux had entered his life. Carrying an enormous, grinning bear she'd marched in and turned his life upside down. She'd looked at him with her big blue eyes, spoken in a voice soft as velvet, and told him there would be no shame in his crying out his inner pain.

Unreal, Patrick repeated in his mind. He'd held on to that big old bear like a lifeline and cried. He hadn't cried since he was eight years old and had fallen out of a tree and broken his arm. But that night with Teddy the tears had flowed, the anguish had come in great sobs until he'd worked it all out, cleansed his soul of all the misery and fear stored there.

The future, he'd then known, was his to do with as he would. It was bright, filled with challenges that were his for the choosing.

And the future had Lux.

As he'd closed the door on the years of football, he'd also ended the chapter in his life of meaningless sex. He wanted more. He wanted a home, family, commitment. He wanted, he loved, Lux Sherwood.

The really fantastic part, he thought, was that Lux had come into his life when he was no longer Acer Mullaney, football star. He was simply Patrick Mullaney, the man. Whatever they had together would be real, honest, not clouded with any doubts that the aura of who he was on Sunday afternoons had attracted a beautiful woman.

Damn it was good, and right, and, he admitted, a dream he'd had tucked away in a dusty corner of his mind. In the past he hadn't really trusted the motives of the women who'd sought him out. There were too many who were interested in the uniform, not caring about the man who wore it. But now there was no uniform, no cheering crowds, no reporters ready to record his every move on and off the field. For him, the lights had been turned off, the fans had gone home, the ball game was over.

And there, standing in the new circle of sunshine that was peaceful, and real, and waiting for him, was Lux.

Oh, how he loved her!

Patrick glanced at the clock, then exchanged the weight for a heavier one. He resumed the leg lifts, his knee screaming for mercy. Sweat rolled off him in rivers.

And Lux? he thought, his breathing now labored from his physical efforts. What was she thinking? Feeling? He had a road to go, he knew that. She'd surrounded herself with people who needed her, to ease the pain of her parents' defection. A pain he didn't even think she realized was deep within her. Those people in need, Sally, Mick, Pete, and now Elizabeth Lux, were like a protective wall she was hiding behind. The way things stood now, he wasn't sure there was room for love to wiggle through a crack in her fortress. Yep, he had a tough road to go.

"But I'll win, Teddy," Patrick gasped, raising

his leg. "This is bigger, more important than any Super Bowl. This is all and everything. This, pal, is Lux Sherwood."

Furry blue number sixteen beamed.

Lux finished cleaning the kitchen, deciding that dried stew resembled concrete. She sank onto a chair at the kitchen table with a glass of milk, and thought of Patrick.

Of course, she mused dryly, who else would she be thinking about? From the moment she'd met him, it seemed, Patrick had been her nearly full-time mental occupation. *He* was the cause of her confusion. *He* was the cause of her jangled nerves. *He* was the cause of the conflicting, jumbled messages coming from her heart and mind.

And he was the cause of desire within her like none she had ever known.

It was Patrick Mullaney who brought the soft smile to her lips when he walked into a room, made her heart do flip-flops, and the warm fuzzy feeling to nestle within her. He was the source of a myriad of emotions tumbling together all at once: excitement, fear, passion, and wondrous yearnings on a purely feminine plane.

He heightened her senses, urging her to touch and be touched, to drink in the male scent of him, feel his steely muscles move beneath her hands. She was acutely aware of her own woman-liness, was infinitely glad she was female; soft, gently curved, smaller boned, to be a perfect coun-terpart to Patrick, the man; hard, rugged-edged, massively built, gathering her to the safe haven of his muscled body with strong arms wrapped pro-tectively around her.

Did it all add up to love?

Was she in love with Patrick "Acer" Mullaney?

Lux sighed. Patrick had tossed their "just friends" program out the window, had demanded, and she'd agreed, to go further, discover what was happening between them. That much she had understood from his sudden, unexpected angry outburst of the previous night. The remainder of what he'd ranted about was a confusing blur. But she did know she had said "yes," that she did wish to find the answer to what was building and growing between them.

But what if she discovered that she loved him? What then? What guarantee was there that Patrick would feel the same way? What safeguard did she have against him breaking her heart, deciding it had been an interesting interlude, that she was refreshing, different from the women he knew, but actually not his type? What if he discovered that, yes, he wanted her, desired her, would be only too happy to make love with her, but he really didn't need her in his life?

Just didn't need her.

Lux pressed her trembling fingers to her lips as tears misted her eyes. She felt as though she could cry for three days straight, and she wouldn't even know what the tears were for!

That was dumb, she told herself. If a person was to have a red nose, puffy eyes, a roaring headache, and the hiccups from a loud and lengthy cry, at least they should know why they were crying. Being confused and frightened by so much happening so quickly with Patrick wasn't enough cause to weep buckets. But she had a sneaky suspicion that if someone looked at her wrong, she'd wail to the rafters. Absurd.

Patrick had cried, she mused. Big, strong Acer Mullaney had cried out his pain, his fear, his frustration over the twist of fate that had ended his football career.

And he'd trusted Lux enough to tell her of his tears.

"Oh, Patrick," she whispered, "what a precious gift that was to give to me. Thank you." He was so dear, sweet, tender, caring. He was gentle, and funny, and thoughtful. He was a ladies' man, a womanizer. He was . . . "That's it. No more of this," she said, getting to her feet. "My brain is turning into scrambled eggs."

Pete shuffled into the kitchen. "Scrambled eggs? I'd love some. Coffee, too, and toast. Having a baby is exhausting. I'll just sit here while you fix breakfast."

"In your ear, Peter," Lux said. She sniffed indignantly, spun around, and stomped out of the room.

"I tried," Pete said to no one. He shrugged and headed for the refrigerator. "You win some, you lose some."

As Lux drove to Warm Fuzzies and Friends, she glanced up at the sky. It was overcast, and thunder rumbled in the distance. The white, fluffy clouds were being chased by dark, threatening ones.

Business, Lux knew, would virtually come to a standstill if it rained. People in the Phoenix area were unaccustomed to driving in inclement weather, and since rain was such an infrequent occurrence they simply didn't venture out if it wasn't necessary, knowing it would soon be sunny again.

Would Patrick come to the store? Or would the

weather or the fatigue from the long hours of the night before keep him at home? Had he paid heavily for overexerting his knee? Was he, now, at that moment, in additional pain because he'd gone to the hospital with her to wait for the arrival of Elizabeth Lux? Oh, that had been such a sweet thing for him to do. And dear, and thoughtful, and . . .

"Don't start *that* list again, Lux Sherwood," she said aloud. She turned on the radio and sang along with the blaring music, managing for the moment to blank her mind of thoughts of Patrick.

When Patrick arrived at Warm Fuzzies and Friends, he found Lux in the office with her nose buried in a stack of papers. He quietly observed her for a long moment, realizing he was gazing at the woman, the only woman, he'd ever loved.

He wanted to shout it from the rooftops, tell the world that he was in love, announce to all and everyone that he wasn't just a set of muscles in a fancy uniform on Sunday afternoons, he was a man. A man with hopes and dreams, the desire to be part of a loving family unit, a husband, and father.

But, he thought dryly, a declaration to the masses of the newly discovered condition of Acer Mullaney's heart would be a bit premature. Due to the fact that he was on shaky ground with said subject of his affections, he'd do well to keep his big mouth shut.

Slow and easy, Mullaney, he told himself. He mustn't rush Lux, or pressure her in any way. She was skittish like a wary colt, obviously unsettled, disturbed by what was taking place in ever-growing intensity between them. Yet there was another part of her, too, that responded to his kiss and touch, gave more of herself whenever he took her into his arms. Yeah, he'd have to go slow and easy, but winning the love of Lux Sherwood would be worth it.

Patrick cleared his throat so as not to startle Lux, who was concentrating totally on the papers she was reading. She looked up in surprise, saw Patrick, and smiled.

Ah, man, he thought, look at that smile, those eyes, that face. Lux was just so damn beautiful.

"Hi," she said softly. Oh, hello, Patrick Mullaney. She'd been waiting for him to come, hoping that he'd come, and she hadn't even realized it. And now he was there; so tall, strong, tanned, and smiling at her. There it was again, the warm fuzzy feeling glowing inside of her, and the urge to fling herself into his arms and be the recipient of his mind-boggling kiss. Hello, hello, hello, Patrick. "How's your knee?"

"Hi, yourself," he said, walking slowly forward. "My knee is fine. You look busy."

"I do?" She blinked. "Oh, I do! I am." She waved the papers in the air. "Orders. Sharon was deluged this morning. These are all orders for different kinds and sizes of animals wearing graduation caps and gowns in various colors. It's incredible, and only just beginning."

"That's great," Patrick said, nodding.

Lux got to her feet, a frown on her face. "It is, but it isn't. How can I get all of these finished on time? I do the hand sewing for every one. Sally has been helping but . . ."

"Whoa," he said, raising his hand. "Calm down. You're getting all shook up."

"I *am* shook up. I only have so many hours in the day, Patrick. I've got a reputation to protect. I've never been late with an order. Never. These toys dressed in caps and gowns won't be of use to anyone *after* graduation."

"It seems to me, Lux, that there must be competent people at the company that does the majority of the sewing. Why can't they just finish them there? Deliver them to you ready to go?"

"No," she said sharply. "I finish them. I need to know they're perfect."

"Couldn't you carefully inspect each one when it arrives here?"

"It wouldn't be the same. Anyone could do a final inspection. Warm Fuzzies and Friends is mine. I need to know that I'm . . ." Her voice trailed off.

"Needed?" he said gently. He went around the desk and stood in front of her. He cupped her neck, slowly stroking the line of her jaw with his thumbs.

"It sounds so foolish," she said. "I don't expect you to understand."

He lowered his head slowly toward hers. "But I do understand." He brushed his lips over hers. "More than you realize." He kissed one corner of her mouth, then the other. "We'll find a solution for this, Lux. Together. We will. You'll see."

His mouth melted over hers, and a soft sigh of pleasure whispered from her lips. He caught the sensuous sound in his mouth as his tongue slid between her lips and explored the sweet darkness within. He moved one hand to her back, the other circled her shoulders as he gathered her to him.

Lux slid her hands up his chest to circle his neck as she savored the feel and taste of Patrick.

Nothing mattered but the moment; not caps and gowns, orders, pressure, lack of time to do it all, nothing. There was only Patrick, his kiss, his taste, the heat that was curling inside her, weaving from him into her. There was only this man, and the desire he evoked, the aching, wonderful want.

"Lux," he murmured, then claimed her mouth once more. This was his woman, his love, his life. The hell with slow and easy. He was going to tell her that he loved her, that she was all and everything to him, that . . . No. No, not yet. She wasn't ready to hear that yet. No. "No . . ." he said, lifting his head. "Lux," he said, his voice gritty with passion, "enough. This is hardly the time or the place."

"Hmm? Oh!" she said, stepping backward. The chair caught her at the back of the knees and she landed on the soft leather with a thud. "Oh!"

Patrick chuckled, then went around to the front of the desk and sat down in the chair opposite it. Lux patted her hair in an obviously nervous gesture, then slowly met his gaze.

"Let's get to the down and dirty," he said.

"I beg your pardon?" she said, her eyes widening.

"Business, Lux. It's time to talk business from a practical standpoint. My courses in college also included time management, efficiency factors, the whole nine yards. Warm Fuzzies and Friends is growing by leaps and bounds, but you're not making the necessary internal adjustments."

Lux laughed. "Why is it that your fancy phrases sound kinky? Internal adjustments?"

"Knock it off," he said, grinning at her. "This is serious."

Her smile faded. "I know. I'm grateful for this

success, Patrick, I truly am. I just don't want to lose control of things, become a mini-factory with no personal touch. I hated having to farm out as much of the work as I have, but now I can't keep up with what's left. There's no way I can hand sew the faces and final seam for all those toys."

"Give more work to Sally."

"She has a new baby to tend to."

"A new baby who will sleep a lot at first. Mick and Sally need every penny they can get their hands on. If you're satisfied with Sally's work, then give her more to do."

"Yes, they do need the money," she said slowly.

Damn, Patrick thought. He hadn't handled that right. She'd slipped out of her role of business-woman to one who needed to be needed.

"Okay," he said. "Now, the faces. Can't you compromise? Have the faces sewn on before the toys are delivered?"

Lux sighed. "Yes, I suppose. I had to do that once when we had a huge order and Sharon was down with the flu. I was so busy out front that I had no time to sew, and there were too many to do in the evenings. I sent them back and had the faces put on."

"And?"

"And they were fine. Very nicely done. All right, Patrick, I see what you're saying." She sighed again. "I'll call and talk to them about it. That would leave only the final seam for me to do."

"For Sally to do."

"Both of us."

"You have a business to run, Lux. Hand sewing is a luxury you can't afford."

"I do it in the evenings."

"Oh? What if I want to see you in the evenings?

Take you to dinner, a movie, a play? Lux, you've reached the point where you don't have to put in twenty-four hour days. I respect the fact that you were willing to do that to get things rolling, but it's not necessary anymore. There are other things in this world besides work. For example, spending time with me."

"I have a social life. I go out on the weekend," she said, lifting her chin.

"How nice for you," he said dryly.

"What is your problem?"

"My problem?" he said, leaning forward. "It's very simple. I want to see you, be with you, and I'll be damned if I'll be put on the shelf like some Warm Fuzzy bear until the weekend because you've got a damn seam to sew."

"They're not damn seams," she said, getting to her feet. "They're important seams. *My* seams. No one touches my seams but me."

Patrick grinned and wiggled his eyebrows. "Talk about kinky."

Lux plopped back down in the chair and glared at him. "Shut up, Patrick Mullaney."

"No. No, I will not shut up because what I'm saying needs to be said. You've worked hard, knocked yourself out. Now it's time to get a better balance in your life. A balance," he said, thumping himself on the chest, "that includes me." He paused. "Who do you see on the weekends for your ever-famous social life?"

"Oh, people," she said, examining her fingernails.

"Male people?" he said, his voice rising. "People in pants?"

Lux burst into laughter. "Oh, for heaven's sake."

"It's a reasonable question," Patrick said, scowling. "I don't want you out with other guys. I don't want you seeing anyone but me."

Lux immediately became serious. "Oh? And you, Patrick? What about all those women that you . . ."

"Cut," he said, slicing his hand through the air. "That's old news. I have no intention of seeing anyone but you. This is important, Lux. We agreed to find out what's happening between us. We can't do that with a bunch of other people in the way." Dammit, he *knew* how he felt about her. He was in love with her, for crying out loud. Slow and easy was one thing. Having her dating other men was another ball game. No way. "Agreed? We only see each other?"

"Oh, well, I . . . I . . . Yes, all right," she said. Oh, why not? she thought, mentally throwing up her hands. If she was going to have her heart smashed to smithereens, she might as well do a royal job of it.

"Fine," he said gruffly. Praise the Lord for small favors. This woman was going to put him in an early grave. "Good. Dinner tonight? Eight o'clock? I'm afraid my knee isn't up to dancing yet, but we can have a nice meal."

"That sounds lovely, Patrick," she said, smiling.

"Great," he said, matching her smile.

They gazed at each other, felt the heat, the crackling sensuality begin to weave its magic spell once again. But neither moved to shatter the moment, to drive back the hazy glow that seemed to settle over them. It was familiar now, theirs. It caused hearts to race and blood to hum in their veins. They ached with the need to reach for each other, be held, touched, kissed. But neither moved.

The telephone rang.

"Oh," Lux gasped. She jumped in her chair as her hand flew to her pounding heart.

Patrick shook his head slightly as if coming out of a trance, then reached for the receiver, noticing that his hand wasn't quite steady.

"Warm Fuzzies and Friends . . . Yes, she is. Just a moment, please." He handed the receiver to Lux. "It's for you."

"Thank you," she said, taking the receiver. Their fingers brushed, and she felt the heat of Patrick's hand travel up her arm, across her breasts, then land with a flutter deep within her. "Lux Sherwood. May I help you?" Was that husky voice hers? "Yes, I see . . . Certainly . . ." She began to write on a pad of paper. "Absolutely. We thank you very much, and I'll get a confirmation out to you today. Good-bye." She slowly replaced the receiver.

"Trouble?" Patrick said. "You're frowning."

"What? Oh, no, not trouble exactly. That was the senior class sponsor from Salt River High School. They want six-inch tigers dressed in purple and gray caps and gowns as favors for the senior prom. Two . . ." She took a deep breath. ". . . two hundred and fifty of them."

Patrick leaned back in his chair, rested his elbows on the arms, and made a steeple of his fingers. "I see."

"All right. Okay," Lux said, smacking the desk with her hand. "Enough is enough. I'll get on the phone and make arrangements for all the special orders for the cap and gown toys to be completely finished before they're delivered. I'll do the final inspection here. Sally can sew seams on the regular stock items. All faces will be done on the outside. If Sally gets busy with Elizabeth Lux, I can pitch in, but as of now I am no longer doing hand sewing."

"Lux, I . . ."

"Don't say anything to me right now, Patrick," she said, getting to her feet. "I'm a breath away from bursting into tears, and that is so ridiculous. My business is flourishing, and I should be shouting with joy. I am, however, so miserable I could cry for a week. Just leave me alone for awhile. Okay? I'm acting like someone who is certifiably insane."

Patrick got to his feet. "No, you're not. I understand. I really do."

"I'm glad *you* do, because *I* don't. I think I'm a nut case. Just . . ." She waved her hand over the desk. ". . . do this paperwork, all right?"

"Yes," he said gently. "I'll place the orders. I'll make arrangements for the finishing work to be done, too. Do you want me to do that?"

"Yes," she said, her voice trembling. "Yes, that would be most helpful. Thank you." She hurried from the room.

Patrick watched her go, resisting the urge to go after her. He shook his head and went around the desk to sit in the chair Lux had vacated.

Ah, Lux, he thought, looking at the door again, he did understand. She was floundering, standing and watching her need to be needed slip through her fingers at Warm Fuzzies and Friends. She, herself, didn't understand her own upset, and she was frightened. He wanted to go to her, hold her, comfort her. He wanted to tell her that he loved her and, yes, *he* needed her.

He needed her as a man in love needs his woman by his side. His need went hand in hand with his love and want of her. It was, he knew, on an entirely different plane from the needs of the store, of Sally, Mick, Pete, and the baby. Why he was suddenly so wise about the complexities of love, he wasn't sure. What he was certain of, was that if he told Lux now that he loved and needed her, it would be a terrible mistake.

"Slow and easy," he said aloud. He had to wait, give her time. To tell her now would be running the risk of her pulling his need for her into a place where it didn't belong. She had to, somehow, come to see that she had used Sally and the others, even Warm Fuzzies and Friends, to ease the pain caused by her parents leaving her.

Then, and only then, Patrick realized, would the ghosts of her past be put to rest, and make room for her to receive his love, then return his love, as it was meant to be.

He wished Lux's grandmother was there to give him some advice. She had been, from what Lux had said, a very special and wise person. But she was gone, and he was alone, fighting for the love of his woman. And he was going to win.

"I hope," he said quietly. "I have to. I just have to."

With a shake of his head and a deep frown on his face, Patrick got to work.

Thunder rumbled across the sky and minutes later a heavy rain began to fall. Patrick glanced up as he saw Lux walk past the office doorway, her arms full of stuffed toys to replenish the shelves in the front.

Just leave her alone, Mullaney, he told himself, then reached for the telephone.

Two hours later, Patrick leaned back in the chair and rotated his neck to loosen his muscles.

"The rain has stopped," Lux said quietly from the doorway. "You've been working very hard, Patrick. Aren't you ready for a break? I could make a fresh pot of coffee."

"No, thanks. It's nearly quitting time."

"Did . . . did you make all the arrangements?"

"Yes."

"Thank you. You certainly are efficient. I appreciate your help."

"Lux . . ."

"I'm fine. Really. I've explained to Sharon about the changes in procedure, and she thinks it's a wonderful new system. She's been telling me that I should delegate things so I can be out front with the customers where I like to be."

"She's right."

"I know. And you're right, too. I can't do it all anymore, it's just too big. I'm sorry I overreacted to the whole thing."

"You don't owe me an apology. I do understand what you're feeling, Lux. This business was like your baby, and it grew up, that's all. You have to know when to let go a bit. It doesn't make you any less . . . needed here. It simply means you're gaining some freedom of time to do what you want to after working so hard for so long."

Lux walked slowly forward. "Freedom of time? What an interesting way to put it." She stopped in front of the desk.

Patrick smiled. "I'm just trying to explain things the way I see them. You know, I'm experiencing this now-famous freedom of time, too. My life has been controlled, in a sense, by football since I was in high school. Grown men, professional athletes, having bed checks during the season when we were on the road. Bed checks, for Pete's sake, to make sure we were all tucked in like good little boys at camp. I reported in when I was told, practiced until I was dying because I was told, ate what I was told. I loved it, I truly did. But now? What a heady feeling! My life is mine to do with as I will."

"Freedom of time."

"Yep," he said, lacing his hands behind his head. "And freedom of choice." *And freedom to love. And he did.* "That's where you are, too, Lux. You've earned it. Enjoy it."

Lux sank into the chair in front of the desk and looked directly at Patrick. "Yes," she said thoughtfully. "I think I'm beginning to get the picture."

Do not, Patrick told himself, *leap across that desk and haul her into your arms. Slow and easy, Mullaney.*

"But, Patrick, what about the Blue Falcons? I mean, you were their star. You took them to the Super Bowl more than once, and won. Don't you worry about how they'll do without you?"

Should he say it? he asked himself frantically. It was risky and might upset her. But her question was custom-made for the answer beating against his brain.

He leaned forward, crossing his arms on the top of the desk as he held her gaze.

"They don't need me, Lux," he said, his voice low.

She stiffened in her chair, her eyes wide. "How can you say that? Of course, they need—"

"No!" he interrupted sharply. "Yeah, I did a good job for them, came through when things were rocky for many years, didn't let them down. But who in the hell would I think I was if I decided I was the only man around qualified to throw a football for the Falcons? No, Lux, they don't need me. They'll move on to the next guy with a strong arm and a cool head, and I'll get on with my own life. I've accepted that, and heaven knows they have."

"But . . ."

"Just the way," he continued, his tone gentler, "you're going to accept that you're not the only one who is capable of sewing smiling faces on toys, and closing seams. It doesn't take anything away from who you are, it gives you a chance to discover even more about yourself. Don't you see that, Lux?"

She looked down at her hands that were clutched tightly in her lap, drew a shaky breath, then finally met his gaze again.

"Yes," she whispered. "I do see. I don't want to, you know, but I do. Oh, Patrick, what's wrong with me? I feel like a frightened child."

Patrick got up and came around the desk, ignoring the grinding pain in his knee from having sat in one place too long. He gripped Lux's upper arms and drew her gently from the chair, pulling her close, and wrapping his arms around her.

"There's nothing wrong with you that time . . ." And love. His love. ". . . won't take care of. Things are changing in your life, that's all. You have every right to be frightened and to cry if you want to. That's what you told me, remember? I was so blown away because of my changes, and you put me back on the right track. You and my buddy Teddy, of course."

Lux lifted her head to smile at him through the tears in her eyes.

"Thank you, Patrick, for being so patient with me," she said. She loved him. "I should have listened to the advice I gave you instead of falling apart." She did! Oh, dear heaven, it was true. She was in love with Patrick "Acer" Mullaney. "Warm Fuzzies and Friends is going to be fine even if I don't sew smiles on chipmunks." She loved him.

"You bet," he said, lowering his head toward hers. He'd won the battle, but the war wasn't over. The victory for this skirmish, though, was his. And Lux's. The two of them, together. He had to be patient, take one step at a time. Slow and easy.

The kiss was not slow.

The kiss was not an easy, lazy, sensuous meeting of lips. It was hard, fast, urgent, and hungry.

She loved him! Lux's mind echoed, and so did her heart.

"Oops," Sharon said, from the doorway.

Patrick slowly lifted his head and glanced over his shoulder at Sharon, not releasing his hold on a now blushing Lux.

"Hi," he said. "You rang?"

Sharon laughed. "My timing is poor. I just wanted to say good night. I'll lock the door on my way out." She flapped her hand at them. "Go back to what you were doing. It looked delicious. I think I'll go home to my hubby and get myself a serving of that stuff. 'Bye, guys." She hurried away.

Patrick looked back at Lux, and they both burst into laughter.

"Caught," he said.

"No joke."

"Ah, Lux, I love it when you laugh." Hell, he loved everything about her. "You're very beautiful, do you know that?"

"Cute, maybe."

"Beautiful. You're cute, too."

"You're crazy."

"I'm hungry, that's what I am. Go home so I can come pick you up to go to dinner. I'll choose the restaurant. Let's go, my sweet, I'm a starving man."

He was a wonderful man, Lux thought, as they left the store. A complex, deep, wonderful man. A ladies' man? She wasn't going to think about that tonight.

Not on the night she'd found the answer, discovered the true depth of her feelings, and knew without a doubt that she was in love with Patrick Mullaney.

Outside, Patrick told Lux he'd see her in record time, then stepped off the curb as she started away in the opposite direction.

"Lux, wait!" a voice called.

Lux turned and inwardly moaned. Seth. She retraced her steps to meet him in front of the store. "Hi," she said.

Out of the corner of her eye she saw that Patrick had opened his car door, but was now standing with his arms folded across the top of the door, observing the scene on the sidewalk.

Seth gripped Lux's shoulders and smiled at her. "I'm glad I caught you, sweetheart. I just received official confirmation of my promotion to assistant vice-president at the bank. Let's go out and celebrate."

"Oh, but I . . ."

"Do you realize what this means?"

Lux frowned. "Not really. What does it mean?"

"We can make our plans for the future, Lux. You and me, together. I'm getting a substantial raise with this promotion which will make it possible for me to provide for you and . . ."

"Oh, now, Seth, wait a minute," she said. "I'm terribly sorry if I ever gave you the impression that I . . ."

The door of Patrick's car was slammed with a resounding thud. Lux cringed. Patrick joined the pair on the sidewalk.

"Just what impression did you think you were giving him, Lux?" Patrick said tightly.

"Lord, you're Acer Mullaney," Seth said. "Lux, you never told me that you knew Acer."

"Oh, well, I didn't know him," she said, "but now I do. Patrick . . . Acer . . . this is Seth."

"Who is obviously under the impression that you two have a future together," Patrick said, a muscle jerking in his jaw. "Would you care to explain that, Ms. Sherwood?"

Lux planted her hands on her hips. "The way you explained your relationship with Brenda What's-her-name? No, thank you."

"There was nothing serious between me and Brenda!" Patrick yelled.

"Well, there's nothing serious between me and Seth, either," Lux said, matching his volume.

"There isn't?" Seth said. "I sure as hell thought there was."

"Oh, Seth, I'm sorry," Lux said. "I was going to talk to you, explain that my feelings just weren't taking the same path as yours were. I didn't mean for you to find out in the middle of an argument here on the sidewalk. I really am terribly sorry."

Seth raised his hands. "Hey, no problem. I knew it was wishful thinking on my part. I was hoping you'd . . . Well, so be it. I'll . . . Um . . . see you around, Lux. Nice meeting you, Acer."

"Yeah, same here," Patrick said.

"Good-bye, Seth," Lux said quietly.

Silence hung heavily in the air as Seth hurried away.

"Well," Patrick finally said, "I obviously owe you an apology. I jumped to conclusions without knowing the real facts."

"Yes, you did, but . . ." Lux turned to look at him. ". . . this had made me realize that I'm guilty of the same thing. I've judged you on the basis of stories I've heard, and pictures I've seen. That was wrong of me, Patrick. I owe you an apology, too."

He smiled. "Let's call it even, okay? I'd say we've learned a valuable lesson here."

"Yes, I think you're right."

"Say, do you think Seth would like to meet Brenda? They might make a terrific couple."

Lux laughed. "Only if Brenda gets a charge out of the prime rate." She started down the sidewalk. "See you at the house, Patrick."

"I'll be right behind you," he said, under his breath. "I'm not losing another minute of this night, Lux Sherwood. Not a one."

Eight

Lux arrived home to find, wonder of wonders, that the locksmith had been there, and the front door was once more in working order. Pete had tacked a large sign to it that read ENTER HERE, and Lux swooshed in with a dramatic flair.

Her regal entrance, however, was not noticed by either Mick or Pete, as they were on the living room floor, their noses buried in papers as they sat surrounded by pieces of white wood.

"Oh," Lux said, coming to an abrupt halt. "What is all that?"

"A crib for Elizabeth Lux," Mick said, not looking up. "I hope. Man, a guy needs an engineering degree to put one of these together."

"We'll figure it out," Pete said. "In ten or twenty years."

Lux laughed. "Well, take your time. You want to do it right."

Mick glanced at her. "We don't have much time. Sally's on the new twenty-four-hours deal. I'm picking her and Elizabeth Lux up tonight after the doc makes his final rounds."

Lux sank onto a chair. "You're kidding. They're sending that teeny, tiny baby home already?"

"Yep," Mick said. "Pete, you're holding that piece upside down."

"But we're not ready for a baby," Lux said. "There's nothing here. They need a lot of . . . stuff."

"Sally made me a list and I went shopping," Mick said. "She'd been planning on doing it this week, had the money set aside, had compared prices, the whole bit. I just had to follow her instructions and go to the right place for the right junk. My Sally is something."

"Oh, well, yes, she is," Lux said, frowning slightly. "I was going to take her shopping and . . . Well, no matter. You're sure you have everything you need? Well, of course, you are. Sally made the list. I didn't realize that she had done all that on her own. I mean, I thought she'd need help."

"Nope," Mick said. "She'd been reading a bunch of books from the library on baby care. You should see her with Elizabeth Lux. She handles her like a pro."

"She does?" Lux said. "Well, that's nice. I guess you have everything under control."

"Yep," Mick said. "Listen, I got my blood test today. The doc is filling out Sally's form, and we get our marriage license in three days. I made an appointment at the courthouse for Friday afternoon at two o'clock. We'd like you and Acer to be there."

"Oh," Lux said. "Well, sure. Patrick is taking me out to dinner tonight. You can tell him when he gets here. Sharon can watch the store. Congratulations, Mickey. You seem very happy."

"If he gets any happier," Pete said, "we'll have to put rocks in his shoes to hold him down. He's floating around. He's been a busy man. By the weekend he'll have a new wife, baby, new job, new place to live, a—"

"What?" Lux said, getting to her feet. "Slow down here. The wife and baby I'm aware of. What about the rest of that list? Mick?"

"It's perfect, Lux," Mick said. "I can't believe it myself. The owner of the club where Pete and I play has a huge house in the foothills. I went by the club today to pick up my check, and we were talking. There's a guest house on his property and my boss is looking for someone to live there and keep the lawn and flowers spiffy. A caretaker. I used to work for a landscaping place, and I know that stuff frontward and backward."

"And?" Lux said.

"He hired me. Sally, the baby, and I are moving into the guest house rent free in exchange for the gardening. Plus, I get a small salary to boot. The guy is great. He agreed to let Pete play as a single during the week, and we'll be a duet on the weekends. That's extra cash for me, but I won't have to leave Sally alone every night. If she can keep on sewing for you, we'll make it. We won't live like high-rollers for now, but we'll make it. Pretty good, huh?"

"Yes, it's . . ." Lux forced a weak smile. ". . . wonderful. I'm very happy for you both. I guess you don't . . . need me for anything."

Mick got to his feet and gave her a hug. "I don't know what we would have done without you all these months, Lux. You've been so generous, so giving. We love you. But you don't have to worry about us anymore because we're going to be fine."

"Of course, you are. Well, Pete, I guess it will just be the two of us rambling around here."

"Well, actually, Lux," Pete said, "I've got a deal cooking, too."

"Oh?" she said, feeling a knot tighten in her stomach.

"The owner of the club said he fired the guy who has been cleaning up because the joker was helping himself to the booze. He offered me the job. There's a small apartment over the club. It's a sweet deal and I grabbed it. I'm moving tomorrow."

"Tomorrow," she repeated, a rushing noise echoing in her ears.

"I ditto what Mick said, Lux. I owe you a lot, and I'm very grateful to you for putting up with me. You'll have your house back, your peace and quiet. From what I see going on between you and Acer, the timing is perfect. You two deserve a little privacy here."

"But . . ." she started.

"Lots of changes going on," Mick said, flopping back down onto the floor. "And all for the good. Our lives are squared away, we all have what we need. Come on, Pete, we've got to figure this crazy thing out. You've got that piece upside down again."

"You all have what you need," Lux whispered.

"What?" Mick said.

"Nothing. I'm going to go take a bubble bath, and get ready for my dinner date with Patrick." She turned and nearly ran from the room.

"It's upside down, dumbbell," Mick said.

"It is not!"

"The clown is standing on his head."

"Oh. It's upside down."

• • •

Lux closed the door to her room, then leaned against it, drawing great gulps of air into her lungs. On trembling legs she moved forward and sank onto the edge of the bed, pressing her hands to her flushed cheeks.

They were all leaving her, she thought frantically. They . . . they just didn't need her. They didn't need her anymore. Oh, please, no, they couldn't go, leave her all alone, and . . .

"Stop it," she said, fighting back her tears. What on earth was the matter with her? She felt as though the bottom were falling out of her world, and she was being hurled into a dark, frightening abyss. She'd had to face the changes at Warm Fuzzies and Friends, and now Sally, Mick, the baby, Pete, everyone was going, leaving her. No! She couldn't handle this, not all at once, not so many changes.

They just don't need me!

"Oh, dear heaven," she whispered, as two tears slid down her cheeks, "what's wrong with me?" Why, why, why did she feel so lost, so terribly frightened? The plans that Mick and Pete had made were good, she should be happy that things were coming together for them. But there was a chilling fear within her, a hollow sense of loss, an urge to run back into the living room and beg, plead with them not to go.

Everything was off balance, wrong, her emotions jumbled and confusing. And, oh, so frightening. They were all leaving, she'd be alone, she . . .

"Patrick," she said, getting to her feet. She was in love with Patrick Mullaney. He'd be there soon, they'd go to dinner, have a wonderful evening. She wouldn't be alone, she'd be with Patrick.

For how long?

Hours, days, weeks? Lux thought miserably. How long would it be before Patrick left her too? Before Patrick didn't need her anymore.

"Dear heaven, I'm falling apart," she said, then went into the bathroom.

She ran water in the tub, sprinkled in rose-scented crystals, and sank into the soothing water with a weary sigh.

Okay, she thought, she was calming down. No, she wasn't. Yes, darn it, she was. She had to, because she was acting like a lunatic. Forget that. She refused to be nuts. It was too absurd.

But, she admitted, there was definitely something wrong with her. She should be deciding what to buy Sally and Mick for a wedding present, what to give to Elizabeth Lux. She'd get a surprise for Pete, too, for his new apartment. Wouldn't that be fun? Sure. Yes.

"No," she said. Why was she acting like this? She'd concentrate on Patrick, and the evening ahead. That's all she could deal with right now. She was going out with the man she loved, the only man she'd ever loved. She was going to have a wonderful time if it killed her!

As Lux dressed, she discovered to her own amazement that she was actually carrying out her plan. When the shadowy gloom began to creep in around her, she pushed it away, refused to acknowledge its presence, and thought of Patrick.

Her dress was a sky-blue-colored silk with a softly draped neckline and full skirt. A silk sash circled her waist and the rich color of the material accentuated her dark hair and fair skin.

She looked, she decided, quite stunning. She felt extremely feminine in her pretty dress, and her spirits were now high, anticipating the hours ahead. Hours with Patrick. Hours with the man she loved.

There was a knock on her bedroom door.

"Yes?"

"Lux?" Pete said. "Acer is here."

"I'll be right there."

She picked up her clutch purse and left the room. At the entrance of the living room she stopped, drinking in the sight of Patrick. In a blazer and cashmere turtleneck, he was magnificent. The jacket was obviously expensive and custom-made, fitting him to perfection, stretching across his broad shoulders, hugging his muscular legs. Lux's heart raced as she scrutinized every detail of him, feeling the now familiar heat of desire rush through her.

Oh, how she loved this man.

He was standing next to Pete as they looked at the assembled crib.

"Seems like a big bed for such a little baby," Patrick said. "Elizabeth Lux will be lost in there."

"That's what I said," Pete said, "but Mick says babies grow fast. This is a great crib. The bars are the regulation distance apart. That's very important, you know."

"No, I didn't know," Patrick said, laughing. "I'm getting a real education about babies here."

"Yeah, well, you never know when you might have to draw on that info. Anyway, Mick is off to the hospital, I've got a date, and . . ." Pete glanced up. ". . . and there's your lady. Hey, Lux, you look terrific."

She smiled and walked forward.

"Terrific," Patrick echoed, his gaze sliding over her. "Sensational. Absolutely beautiful."

"Thank you," she said. "You're rather dashing yourself."

"Speaking of dashing, I'm gone to the showers," Pete said. "Take a gander at this crib, Lux. Is that expert work or what? We even got the clown right side up. Well, have a nice evening. See ya later." He left the room.

"Hello," Patrick said, his voice low. "I meant it, Lux. You're beautiful."

"So are you," she said softly.

Patrick frowned. "Are you okay?"

"What do you mean?"

"Pete told me about his plans, and Mick and Sally's plans. I was really surprised, so I can imagine how you felt. I'm sure it's upsetting for you that they're all leaving at the same time. You're facing a great many changes in your life all of a sudden."

"Yes, well," she said breezily, "it happens that way sometimes, doesn't it? Things go plodding along, then . . . swoosh . . . everything changes. Goodness, I'm hungry. I should offer you a drink, but I'll be terribly rude and suggest we go to the restaurant. We can even exit through the front door. What a classy place this is."

No way, Patrick thought, following Lux out of the house. He wasn't buying her lighthearted mood for a second. She was wired, tense, talking too fast, and there was an unnatural flush on her cheeks. He knew exactly how she felt about everyone moving out of the house. Lux was convinced that she wasn't needed anymore.

"Isn't it a lovely night?" Lux said, as they drove away from the house. "The rain has made the air so fresh, and the stars are gorgeous, like diamonds."

"Yep," Patrick said. Okay, they'd play it her way for now. She wasn't fooling him one iota, but he'd go along with it. He'd wait, watch, stay alert. He'd be there for her. Because he loved her.

The restaurant was one of Phoenix's finest. Fashioned after a Swiss chalet, it was a popular attraction to the people living in the valley of the desert because it had an aura of fantasy about it. The waitresses and waiters were dressed in authentic Swiss clothes, and every detail of the decorating enhanced the image of being tucked away high on a mountain in Switzerland.

Lux was enchanted. Patrick watched her as she looked around, her blue eyes sparkling with excitement, a smile on her face.

This was what Lux deserved, Patrick decided, unable to conceal his own smile. She should be carefree and happy, embracing life, ready to experience new things, eager to receive love, should it touch her heart.

Lux Sherwood should not, he thought adamantly, be held in the iron grip of painful ghosts from her past. She was too young, vital, too beautiful, to walk in the shadows. She was sunshine and flowers with her whole future in front of her. A future, he was determined, that would be spent with him.

After they had ordered dinner, Lux chattered on about the charming atmosphere of the restaurant. Patrick commented at all the right places, smiled and nodded, watched her carefully for any signs of distress. He saw none. She was, he surmised, totally caught up in the fantasyland feeling of the room.

Half listening to what she said, Patrick turned his thoughts inward. He had only one weapon against Lux's ghosts. His physical strength meant nothing. His agility meant nothing. His intelligence meant nothing. It was as though he'd been stripped bare of his natural attributes, and left with only one thing with which to do battle.

His love.

It would have to be stronger than the ghosts, because now, he knew, Lux really didn't even know they were there. But as Lux faced the changes at the store, then watched as Mick and the others moved away, the ghosts would gather power. They were a mighty foe, but Patrick intended to win.

The time had come, he knew without doubt, to tell Lux he loved her. Tonight was the night.

"Is your dinner all right?" Patrick asked, pulling himself from his thoughts.

"Delicious. Thank you for bringing me here, Patrick. I've heard about this place, but I've never come. It's wonderful."

He smiled. "If one little Swiss-looking restaurant can make your eyes sparkle like that, I think I'll take you to the real Switzerland."

"Oh, okay," she said, laughing. "Shall we head for Switzerland right after dinner?"

His smile widened. "Absolutely. We'll go in my private jet, of course. I'll call ahead and have the servants open my chalet, and put roses in every room for you."

"Perfect. Oh, I must take my maid with me. She'd be dreadfully disappointed if I left her behind."

"No problem. I'll hire a nanny for the children so we can steal away for some private time."

Lux blinked. "Children?"

Patrick's smile faded and his voice was low when he spoke. "Ours. Our children, yours and mine."

The waiter approached the table before Lux was forced to respond. Their children? her mind echoed. Oh, well, Patrick really didn't mean anything by that. They'd been fantasizing, acting silly, playing a fun, make-believe game.

"Dessert this evening?" the waiter said. He was pushing a three-tiered glass cart containing a variety of fancy, delicious-looking desserts.

"Oh," Lux said, "they're all so beautiful, just like pictures in a magazine."

Patrick chuckled. "Would you like one of each?"

"Don't tempt me," she said, smiling. "I'll have the cherry cheesecake, please."

"Chocolate mint pie for me," Patrick said.

"Certainly," the waiter said. "And coffee?"

"Yes, please," Patrick said, nodding.

The desserts were placed in front of them, and Lux stared at the luscious treat. Dark cherries were nestled on top of the rich cheesecake, the cherry sauce dribbling down the sides. As the waiter poured their coffee, Lux peered across the table at Patrick's dessert. A mound of whipped cream sat on top of the chocolate mint pie, slivers and curls of dark chocolate decorating the white topping.

"Enjoy your dessert," the waiter said, then moved away.

"No doubt about it," Lux said, her gaze still riveted on Patrick's pie.

"Hey," he said, grinning, "this one is mine. Want to trade?"

"Heaven's, no," Lux said, pulling her plate closer to her. "I'd protect this with my life." She picked up her fork, took a bite, and closed her eyes as she savored the enticing flavors.

Patrick watched her, then took a bite of his pie. "Mmm, good," he said. "Interesting, isn't it?"

Lux's eyes popped back open. "Interesting?"

He looked directly into her eyes and his voice was deep and rumbly when he spoke. "Special things are worth waiting for, don't you think?

This dessert is . . . an experience, a happening, a very special event. Anything that falls under those categories is definitely worth waiting for, don't you agree, Lux?"

Patrick Mullaney was no longer talking about cherry cheesecake and chocolate mint pie, Lux thought wildly. The sensual glow in his eyes emphasized the double meaning of his words, and the frisson that danced along her spine announced that her body, as well as her mind, understood.

"Yes, Patrick," she said, hardly breathing, "special experiences are most definitely worth waiting for."

"I was sure," he said, his voice seeming to drop an octave lower, "that you felt that way."

You'd better believe it, Mullaney, Lux thought. She was, however, going to be embarrassed to pieces if she fainted dead out in her cheesecake.

Patrick slowly shifted his gaze back to his pie, and Lux remembered to breathe. They ate their desserts. The spell was broken, but a heightened sexual awareness nearly crackled in the air.

A short time later, Patrick assisted Lux into the car and they were driving away from the restaurant. The star-studded sky had once more been covered by rain clouds, and thunder rumbled in the distance like a lonely drummer.

"Would you like to go to my place to listen to some music?" Patrick said. "It's still early."

"Yes, music would be lovely," Lux said. She didn't want the evening to end, not yet, not so quickly. Even Cinderella had been with her prince until midnight. And Lux was with the man she loved. "Have you ever really been to Switzerland, Patrick?"

"Yes."

Lux shifted in her seat to face him. "Tell me

about it. What are the Swiss people like? Were you in a real chalet that looked like that restaurant? What was everyone wearing?"

"Whoa," Patrick said, laughing. "Okay, let's see . . ."

Lux was oblivious to the heavy traffic and the increased thunder as Patrick told her in great detail about the enchanting things he'd seen in Switzerland. There was a fleeting thought in her mind as to whether he'd taken a woman with him to the fairy-tale land, but then she dismissed it as unimportant. It didn't matter, she decided, because Patrick was with *her* now, and she loved him.

She was still smiling as they entered his house and he led her into the den. He turned on one softly glowing lamp.

"Brandy?" he said.

"Yes, thank you."

"Have a seat."

Lux settled onto the sofa where she'd put Teddy the first day she'd met Patrick. Her smile suddenly felt false, sewn in place like the one permanently attached to Teddy. She was, she realized, registering a flutter of nervousness in the pit of her stomach. Her senses were crowded by Patrick's presence in the room, her skin seeming to tingle as a rush of heat coursed through her.

Tonight, this night, Lux knew, held a magic. She was alone with the only man she'd ever loved. And she wanted him. She wanted to become one with him, not thinking of the future or the tomorrows, just holding fast to the moment, cherishing it.

Patrick sat down next to her, and Lux jumped in surprise. As she accepted her brandy snifter she saw that he'd removed his jacket and tie. Soft music drifted through the air. She took a deep swallow of brandy, then gasped as the fiery liquor burned her throat.

"Easy there," Patrick said. "That's potent stuff. Just sip it." He paused. "Am I making you nervous?"

"No, no. No," she said, then took a sip of brandy. "Not at all."

Patrick frowned and placed his glass on the coffee table. He took Lux's from her, set it next to his, then cradled one of her hands between both of his. He looked directly into her eyes.

The seconds ticked away.

Was this the wrong night? Patrick warred with himself. Beneath Lux's sunny exterior was her fear and upset over all the changes taking place in her life. Was she really thinking clearly, or was she still on the edge, refusing for now to face the fact that Mick and the others were leaving, that her role at Warm Fuzzies and Friends was now different? Should he wait to tell her of his love for her?

No, his mind thundered. If he did, then the ghosts of the past would gain strength as she realized that things were not to be the same in her life. He had to tell her *now*, stake a claim on his place in her existence, push the ghosts into oblivion and crush them into dust. Lux Sherwood was his!

"Lux," he said, his voice slightly husky, "I want to talk to you." Maybe, he thought quickly, he should give her a chance to discuss her fears about the changes taking place. Yeah, good plan. "Lux, listen, I realize you're upset about everyone leaving your house. You know, giving the impression that they don't need you anymore. Plus, you're having to do things differently at the store and . . . Would you like to sort it out? I'm here, you know. I want to help."

"Thank you, Patrick, but there really isn't anything to discuss. Facts are facts, and . . ." She shrugged. ". . . I have to accept them as they are."

Damn, he thought, she wasn't looking deep inside herself, was taking it all at face value. That was wrong. It was going to catch up with her and . . .

"Was that what you wanted to talk to me about, Patrick?"

"What? Oh, yes. I mean, no. No, there's something else, too."

"What is it?"

Lord, he'd never done this before, he thought. How did a man tell a woman that he loved her? He should say it romantically, with flowery words. With his luck, he'd probably open his mouth and say, 'I'm crazy 'bout you, baby. Love ya, ya know what I mean? Whata ya say we get it on?' Oh, cripe.

"Patrick?"

"What? Oh. Lux, I . . . I . . . Oh, hell, Lux, I love you," he blurted out. Wonderful. Just super. That was as romantic as yesterday's oatmeal.

Lux blinked, opened her mouth, closed it, then blinked again. "I beg your pardon?"

"I love you," he said gently. "I truly do. Something happened to me the minute you walked in here with Teddy. You've felt it grow, too, and we agreed we'd try to discover what it was. Well, now I know. I love you. I've fallen very deeply in love with you, Lux, and I felt it was time to tell you."

"Oh, Patrick," she said, flinging her arms around his neck, "I love you, too."

"What?" He moved her back to see her face.

"I do. I love you, but I never dreamed that you . . . Oh, my."

"Ah, Lux," he said, then brought his lips to hers.

She loved him? his mind echoed. She did? Or did she? She was feeling alone and lonely, frightened by all that was going on, knew everyone was leaving her. Did she truly love him or had she jumbled her emotions up like a jigsaw puzzle?

Lux leaned into him, returning his kiss in total abandon.

Think, Mullaney! Patrick ordered himself. He had to look at the facts, sort this through.

Lux's breasts crushed against his chest as her tongue met his in the sweet darkness of her mouth.

The hell with it, Patrick thought hazily. He loved this woman. He needed, he wanted this woman. This was Lux, and she was his!

With a groan, he wrapped his arms tightly around her, and the kiss intensified. All rational thought fled Patrick's mind, and he only felt. Felt Lux. Tasted her, inhaled her intoxicating, feminine aroma. Blood pounded in his veins, and heat gathered low in his body, his manhood surging with his want, his aching need.

"Lux," he murmured, drawing air into his lungs. Then he took possession of her mouth once more.

Patrick loved her, Lux's heart sang. Oh, dear heaven, how was this possible? How could it be that he loved her as she did him? Was this real, or only another part of this magical, fanciful night? No, it was real, she knew that. She'd seen it in his beautiful brown eyes, heard it in his voice. Patrick loved her.

"I want you," he said, close to her lips. "I want to make love with you."

"Yes," she whispered. "Oh, yes, Patrick."

He got to his feet, then took her hand to pull her up next to him. He held her close, burying his face in her fragrant, silky hair. His hands roamed over her back, then down to the slope of her buttocks, nestling her to him.

"Can you feel how much I want you?" he said, his voice raspy. "Only you."

"Yes."

"We're going to be fantastic together."

She tilted her head back to look up at him. "I love you, Patrick Mullaney."

He brushed his lips over hers, then circled her shoulders with his arm, led her from the room, and down the hall to his bedroom.

The drapes were open and the sky was alive with crackling lightning that sent silvery flashes over the expanse. The heavens rumbled and the rain started, beating against the roof and windows in a wild torrent. Lux shivered.

Patrick crossed the room and closed the drapes, repeating the process on the other windows, then turned on a small lamp on a desk against the far wall. He walked slowly toward Lux.

"I've shut out the world," he said, stopping in front of her. He framed her face in his large hands. "There's only the two of us. Nothing else is important right now except what we're about to share. I love you, Lux."

Lux couldn't speak as tears caught in her throat. Desire swirled within her as tempestuous as the storm beyond the windows. Patrick lowered the zipper of her dress, then drew the sash free. The rich material fell in a pool at her feet. A wave of dizziness washed over her, and she was vaguely aware of him removing her remaining clothes. She stood naked before him.

"Oh, my Lux, you're so beautiful." He filled his palms with her small, firm breasts, stroking the nipples with his thumbs.

Lux sighed with pleasure, then reached for the waistband of his sweater. Her hands were trembling, and refused to perform the simple task. Patrick smiled at her gently, then quickly shed his clothes, removing the brace from his knee in the process. Lux's gaze swept over him, inch by inch.

"Oh, Patrick," she said, meeting his gaze.

That was all she said, just "Oh, Patrick." There was such awe and wonder in her voice that Patrick felt more masculine, more aware of his own body than he ever had in his life. And very, very aware of the feminine loveliness of Lux.

He moved to the bed, swept back the blankets, then extended his hand to her. Without hesitation she came to him, placing her hand in his. They stretched out on the cool sheets, close, so close, together.

It was a time of discovery. It was touching, kissing, whispering their declarations of love. Lux's last trace of nervousness vanished as she savored the sensual promise of all that was Patrick. Her fingers tangled in the curly hair on his chest, feeling the steely muscles beneath. He dipped his head to draw the bud of one breast deep into his mouth, and she thought she would die from the sheer beauty of the sensations rocketing through her.

The rain beat against the windows as if demanding entry, but neither noticed. Lux saw only Patrick; Patrick saw only Lux, and passions soared. His lips left her breast to claim her mouth as his hand slid over the flat plane of her stomach, then lower, lower. Lux's eyes widened.

"It's all right," he said, his voice gritty with desire. "Trust me. Trust me, Lux."

"Yes, I do."

His touch was bold, but gentle, teaching her so much, giving her so much. Lux clutched the sheet in her hands as though afraid she'd be swept away in a tide of passion.

"Oh. Oh, Patrick, I . . ."

"Yes, yes, you're fine, you're wonderful. Oh, you're so beautiful. Don't fight what you're feeling. This is for you, Lux."

His fingers were instruments of exquisite sweet torture like nothing Lux had ever known. The heat, the pressure built within her, urging her on, making her ache for more.

"Patrick, please!"

He claimed one breast again, sucking hard. She arched upward, a cry escaping from her lips. Her body tightened, pulsed, then seemed to shatter into a million brightly colored pieces. She went limp, closing her eyes as she felt herself come slowly back together, each bright section shimmering from the ecstasy of where she had been.

"Look at me," Patrick said quietly.

She lifted her lashes. "I've never felt so . . . But what about you? Oh, Patrick, you didn't take, you only gave."

"My turn is coming. I'm going to come to you, Lux, move into you, bring you all that I am."

"Yes."

He teased and tantalized, stroked and caressed, until she was nearly sobbing with the want of him. His muscles trembled from forced restraint until he could bear no more, and he rose above her.

"I love you, Lux."

He filled her.

She sighed.

Deeper.

They were one. Meshed. Together.

And Lux's heart nearly burst with love.

The tempo began, slowly at first, then faster, perfectly matched. Their bodies were slick with the heat of passion as they reached higher, thundering like the heavens above them, pounding like the wild rain. Then . . .

"Patrick!"

"Oh, Lux!"

The colors flashed like the lightning as they were hurled into the place of beauty they had sought. They hovered there, savoring, memorizing, not wishing to return. Slowly, they floated back.

Patrick moved away, tucked Lux close to his side, then drew the blankets over them. Only then did he realize that his knee was burning with pain, protesting what he had pushed it to do. He ignored it as he gently stroked Lux's back.

"Lux?"

"Oh, Patrick, that was the most beautiful experience of my life. Thank you."

He chuckled. "Thank you? Well, okay. Then *I* thank *you*. I also love you. We were fantastic together just as I knew we would be."

"I didn't know it could be so . . . I mean, I haven't had much experience and . . ."

"And you're very rare, very special, and very, very mine."

She sighed, a contented, sated, happy-sounding sigh. "Yes."

"Will you stay the night? I want to wake up next to you in the morning. Everyone at your house will understand, don't you think?"

"Yes." She yawned. "Yes, I'll stay."

"Good. Go to sleep. I'll hold you right here in my arms."

"So nice. I love you, Patrick." Her voice grew faint as sleep claimed her. "I need you so much, Patrick. And . . . and you love me . . . need . . . me."

Patrick stiffened, every muscle in his body tensing, causing his knee to tremble from the increased pain. Lux's sleep-drugged words screamed in his mind.

Love . . . Need . . . Need . . . Love.

What had she meant, really meant, deep within her? he wondered frantically. Were her need and love intertwined on the proper plane where his were for her? Or was the need in Lux held in the fist of the ghosts, pulling him, their love for each other, her need to be needed, into the murky shadows? Was he, then, to be the replacement for Mick and the others, the one to fill the void made by the changes at Warm Fuzzies and Friends?

No!

It mustn't be that way. It was wrong, he raged. But damn, how was he to know the truth when there was every chance that Lux herself didn't know what was real?

"Dammit," he whispered.

The pain in his knee demanded his attention, and he moved carefully from the bed, making sure he didn't disturb Lux. The medicine cabinet in his bathroom had no aspirin, and he went down the hall to the gym. He flicked on one light, found the aspirin, and swallowed two. He was limping badly as he recrossed the room.

He stopped and looked at the big, blue bear.

"Lux is here, Teddy," he said quietly. "Here in

this house, in my bed, where she belongs. I made sweet love with my Lux, just as I'd dreamed. I told her I love her, and she said she loves me."

Patrick ran his hand down his face.

"But, Teddy? Am I kidding myself? Have the ghosts already won? Am I beaten? And, Teddy, how am I supposed to know the truth?"

Patrick shook his head and hobbled from the room, turning off the light as he went. Lightning zigzagged through the storm clouds, casting an eerie glow over the room from the skylight in the ceiling.

In the unnatural luminescence, it appeared as though Teddy were frowning.

Nine

On Friday afternoon, Lux sat next to Patrick in the sports car as they drove to the courthouse for Sally and Mick's wedding. Lux's mind drifted back over the week, pictures floating in her mind like a misty, sensuous movie.

Desire hummed deep within her as she recalled awakening on Wednesday morning to find Patrick leaning on his arm and smiling down at her. Without speaking, he had claimed her mouth in a searing kiss, and the journey of ecstasy had begun. No words were spoken as they reached for each other, touching, stroking, igniting to a flame their passion which had still been a glowing ember from the night before.

When they could hold back no longer, Patrick had moved over her and into her with a powerful thrust that had taken her breath away. Once again they sought and found the place of the brilliant colors, and were flung into the rapture together. They lingered, then drifted back with sated sighs of contentment.

"Oh, my," Lux whispered, feeling the warm flush on her cheeks as she relived the crystal-clear memories.

The movie in her mind played on.

The remainder of the week had rushed by in a flurry of excitement and activities. The fact that Patrick brought Lux home early each morning so she could shower and change in time to go to Warm Fuzzies and Friends caused no censure to be passed. Sally beamed. Mick winked at her. And Pete gave her a brotherly pat on the head. Lux would have felt delightfully sophisticated if only she hadn't blushed crimson.

"We're here," Patrick said, bringing Lux from her reverie as he parked the car. "I wonder if Mick will pass out like he did the night Elizabeth Lux was born."

Lux laughed, then smoothed the skirt of her pale yellow silk dress. Patrick was wearing a gray suit and tie with a pale yellow shirt and, she decided they were a gorgeous couple.

They met the others at the designated place. Sally wore an ice blue dress and was, Lux mused, absolutely glowing. Mick and Pete were in dark suits, Elizabeth Lux was decked out in a tiny, pink dress and bonnet and was wrapped in a delicate white shawl.

"Nervous?" Patrick asked Mick.

"Of course not," Mick said, fiddling with the knot of his tie.

Pete rolled his eyes.

Moments later they were ushered into the judge's chambers where a gray-haired, smiling man in his official robe greeted them. Sally handed the baby to Lux.

"Friends," the judge started, "we are gathered here today to unite in matrimony . . ."

Oh-h-h, Lux thought, as tears misted her eyes, it was just so beautiful. Sally and Mick were pledging their love for all time, through the good and bad, for richer, for poorer. They would stand together, and with them would be this wonderful little baby. Oh, how glorious it would be to say those vows with Patrick Mullaney.

No wonder people cried at weddings, Patrick thought. This was heavy-duty stuff. This was forever. This was what he wanted with Lux. What was Lux thinking as she watched this ceremony? Did she see herself saying the forever vows with him? Or was her mind centered on the fact that Sally, Mick, the baby, Pete, didn't need her anymore?

Patrick slid a glance at Lux, and smiled; a gentle smile, a tug-at-his-heart smile. Tears slid down Lux's cheeks as she jiggled the baby. Lux had a wistful expression on her face, and was obviously very moved by what she was witnessing. There were no ghosts spoiling this special moment.

Patrick reached in his pocket for a handkerchief, then took Elizabeth Lux from Lux's arms. He settled the baby in the crook of his arm and pressed the handkerchief into Lux's hand. She gave him a smile of gratitude. Patrick looked down at the baby, who was staring right back at him.

Yes, he reaffirmed in his mind, he wanted it all, with Lux.

After the wedding, Patrick invited everyone to a late lunch at an expensive restaurant, and the champagne flowed.

That night, Patrick received a call from his agent reminding him he was due in Los Angeles the next day for his annual visit and speech at a home for handicapped children. Both Hammer and Patrick were patrons of the home, giving their time and money, and both were scheduled to appear.

Patrick became extremely agitated at the prospect of leaving Lux, and while she felt very loved that he didn't want to make the trip, she sensed something else; there was an underlying tension about him, and she often looked up to find him studying her intently.

She had spent Saturday working at Warm Fuzzies and Friends, then caring for Elizabeth Lux while Sally and Mick arranged their belongings in the guest house that was to be their new home. Pete had already moved to his apartment.

When Patrick called late Saturday night, Lux had already been asleep, the busy days and, oh, so deliciously busy nights, having finally caught up with her. She vaguely recalled mumbling that she was fine, sleepy but fine, and was counting the hours until his return on Monday. With that, she'd hung up and gone back to sleep.

At dawn on Sunday, the insistent fingers of consciousness tugged at Lux, and she reluctantly released her hold on her lovely cocoon of sleep. Without opening her eyes, she reached across the expanse of bed for Patrick, patting the area next to her until it registered in her foggy brain that he wasn't there. Now fully awake, she rolled onto her back and opened her eyes.

Suddenly she stiffened, lying perfectly still and listening. Listening to nothing. There wasn't a sound in the big old house. She was alone, totally alone.

Because everyone had left her.

Lux waited. She waited for the chill of fear to clutch her soul, the knot to tighten in her stomach, the hated message to beat painfully against her brain.

They just didn't need her anymore.

That was the message that would assault her, cause her throat to ache with unshed tears, her heart to race in fear. Any second now, it would scream against her mind and make her wish to flee in panic.

But the message never came.

She felt her tightened muscles relax, then her thoughts traveled back in time. She saw herself as a little girl, old enough at last to wonder where her parents were, why they weren't a family like all of her friends.

She heard the gentle words of her grandmother explaining that Lux's mother and father had a wanderlust spirit and answered to the call of the endless stretches of highways.

She could feel the warmth of her Gran's love wrapping around her, assuring her that Lux's parents' leaving was not the little girl's fault. Gran loved her, she had said, but first and foremost Lux must love, like, and respect herself, be complete, whole, happy in order to love others in return. She mustn't ever forget that, Gran had said. Not ever.

But Lux had forgotten.

As she lie staring up at the ceiling, alone in her bed, alone in her house, Lux knew that as she'd grown up, she'd slowly forgotten those words spoken with such gentle wisdom and loving care.

When Gran had died, she realized, Lux had floundered, lost touch with those wise words entirely, covered them with the heavy dust of fear and loneliness. She'd poured her energies into Warm Fuzzies and Friends, proving her usefulness, her purpose for being. She'd opened her heart and her home to Mick, Pete, and Sally, telling herself they needed her desperately, that they simply couldn't function properly without her.

But that wasn't true. They had left her for new lives and better times. And it was good. They still needed her friendship, just as she did theirs, but now it was as it should be: adults meeting adults in a normal give and take.

"Dear heaven," Lux whispered, as tears misted her eyes, "what have I done?" Somehow, she now knew, as Gran's words had been buried in dust, so had the ghosts of her parents' defection. While the words had been forgotten, the ghosts had grown stronger, fed by the doubts the darkness provided. They had held her in a fist of fear.

It was all so clear now, Lux thought. She'd brought the ghosts forward, faced them, forced them into the sunshine where they couldn't survive.

And they were gone. Forever.

Ringing as clear as bells, she heard once more Gran's words.

And there in the silent house, Lux Sherwood felt the greatest peace she had ever known.

She did, indeed, love, and like, and respect herself. She was proud of her accomplishments, was whole, complete within herself. She was free to face the future, free of the ghosts of the past.

And free to love Patrick "Acer" Mullaney.

"Oh, Patrick," she said, as tears slid down her cheeks, "what we have is real! It's honest, and true, and wonderful. I love you, Patrick Mullaney."

She threw back the blankets and got to her feet, bursting with energy, happiness, the joy of being alive and in love. And then she stopped statue still.

"Thank you, Gran," she whispered. "Thank you very, very much."

Through the hours of the day, Lux's smile was firmly in place. She cleaned the house from front door to back, rearranged the furniture, and washed all the windows. She swept the dusty corners of her home just as she'd done to her once troubled mind. Her house sparkled, and so did her eyes . . . as she thought of Patrick.

Lux ate dinner, then indulged in a long, lei-surely bubble bath. She pulled on a soft velour robe and curled up in the corner of the sofa with a book, registering a rush of relief that there wasn't a box of toys sitting next to her waiting for smiling faces to be sewn into place. She lost herself in the story she was reading, and the hours ticked by.

Just after ten o'clock, a knock sounded at the front door. Lux jumped in surprise, dropping the book onto the floor in the process. She padded barefoot to the door and stood close to it.

"Who is it?"

"Patrick."

"Patrick? Patrick! "Patrick! But you weren't due back until tomorrow."

"Dammit, Lux, open the door."

"Oh! Yes, of course." She flung the door open.

Before she could speak further, Patrick limped into the room, a deep frown on his face. He sank onto the sofa and clutched his knee with both hands. Lux shut the door and hurried to stand in front of him.

"Why are you back early?" she asked. "What's wrong with your knee? You're limping so badly. Would you like some aspirin?"

"Yeah," he said gruffly.

Lux hurried to get the pills and a glass of water, then returned to the living room. She sat down next to Patrick and watched him anxiously as he swallowed the aspirin and drained the glass of water.

"What happened?" she said, after he'd plunked the glass onto the end table.

"I was on my feet too long over there. Then they screwed up my plane reservations and stuck me in economy. I needed the room in first-class to stretch my leg out."

"But you said you weren't coming back until tomorrow."

He turned to look at her, his dark eyes flashing. "I asked Hammer to cover the final banquet for me because I was going out of my mind."

"I don't understand."

He gripped her shoulders with his strong hands. Lux's eyes widened.

"I was worried sick about you, Lux. Dammit, I was going nuts picturing everyone moving out of here, leaving you alone. I saw you crying, being so frightened, telling yourself that no one needed you. When I talked to you on the phone last night, you were so out of it I couldn't tell where your head was."

"Oh, but I—"

"All the way back on the plane I thought about you, us, what we have together. I tried to tell myself that everything was fine, we loved each other, had our whole future together to plan. I repeated it in my mind over and over, then finally admitted it was a crock."

"What?" Lux whispered. "What are you saying?"

He gave her a small shake. "It's no good, don't you see that? I won't be a substitute for your parents, or for Mick and the others. I was willing to fight for you, Lux, but I don't know how! I was scared to death to leave town in fear that the ghosts would win while I was away. Your ghosts, your need to be needed, are so damn big, tough, and I don't know how to beat them. I just can't do this anymore."

"Patrick, please, listen to me. I know about the ghosts, I know that I—"

"What?" he said, his voice ominously low. "Do you also know that your parents leaving you caused deep scars inside you, a void? Do you know that you tried to fill that void with Sally, Mick, and Pete?"

"Yes, I—"

"Damn you," he yelled, getting to his feet. He clutched his knee for a moment, then straightened. "You knew?" He laughed, a harsh, bitter-sounding laugh. "My God, you're incredible. You had it all figured out, didn't you? Just put poor beat-up Acer Mullaney in the empty slot in your life. Out with the old, in with the new. Telling me that you loved me was a nice touch. And making love with me? I've got to hand it to you, Lux, you give your program your all. It was quite a game plan, and it worked . . . for a while. But now it's over."

Lux jumped to her feet. "How dare you say those things," she said, her voice shrill. "How dare you cheapen what we shared."

"Me?" he said, splaying his hand on his chest. "You used me, Lux Sherwood. You knew what you were doing. You knew about your ghosts, your fears. You were perfectly content to live with them as long as your need to be needed was satisfied. And there I was, just sitting on the bench, waiting to be sent into the game. Well, guess what? I quit!" He turned and started toward the door, one hand spread on his thigh as he hobbled forward.

"Patrick, don't go. You don't understand," Lux said, tears echoing in her voice.

He opened the door and turned to look at her. Pain beyond the physical settled in the rich, dark pools of his eyes, and there was a weary, defeated quality to his voice when he spoke.

"You're wrong," he said, so low that Lux could hardly hear him. "I understand only too well." He appeared as though he were going to say more, then his shoulders slumped, and he shook his head. "Good-bye, Lux," he said, then left the house and closed the door behind him with a quiet click.

"Patrick?" she whispered. "Patrick?" she said louder. "Patrick 'Acer' Mullaney," she hollered, "you giant economy-size dope, you come back here and let me explain. You've got it all backwards. And furthermore, I . . ." Her voice trailed off, and a sob caught in her throat, ". . . I love you with every breath in my body," she said softly. "It's real, Patrick. I swear to you that my love is real. Oh, just . . ." She threw up her hands. ". . . dammit."

She sank onto the sofa, buried her face in a pillow, and wept.

Patrick was gone. Angry and hurt, without having given her the chance to tell him that he'd been right, but now he was wrong, and . . .

Lux sat bolt upward, dropped the throw pillow to her lap, and dashed the tears from her cheeks, her mind racing.

Patrick had understood, sensed, seen, the depths of her inner turmoil, her ghosts, she realized, long before she, herself, had comprehended what was taking place deep within her. Patrick had known because he cared enough to embrace every facet of her being, the total woman, the good and the bad. Patrick had known because that was how much he truly loved her. His was the forever and ever kind of love, the forsaking all others, acceptance including the flaws, until death parted them.

His was a once-in-a-lifetime kind of love.

And she had no intention of losing him.

How, Lux wondered, did one try to talk to a furious, hurt Irishman, who had pride as wide as his broad shoulders, and who felt he had been used and betrayed by the woman he loved? How? Very carefully, if one valued one's life.

Lux got to her feet and began to pace the floor. But, darn it, she thought, he hadn't given her an opportunity to get a word in edgewise. She'd wanted to tell him that she'd looked deep within herself, remembered Gran's words, had found and destroyed the ghosts. She'd wanted to tell Patrick Mullaney that her love for him was every bit as rich and real as his was for her. But he hadn't given her a chance!

That had been, now that she thought about it, extremely rude. Not one bit nice. And if she wasn't so sad, so incredibly miserable about the fact that he'd left her, she'd be rip-roaring angry, mad as . . . as all get out.

"Oh-h-h," she moaned, then sniffled. Sad was obviously winning the debate over mad. Her heart was wobbly . . . Yes, wobbly . . . close to shattering into a million pieces. "Oh-h-h."

No! she thought suddenly, stopping in the middle of the room. She knew as well as she knew her own heart and soul that Patrick truly loved her.

Their love was rare, special, beautiful.

And worth fighting for!

And she would.

Somehow.

With a sigh that was definitely shaky, Lux turned out the light, shuffled down the hall, and went to bed. Then, because she was still just so very sad, she cried herself to sleep.

By two o'clock the next afternoon, Lux knew that Patrick wasn't coming to Warm Fuzzies and Friends. Intellectually she had known he wouldn't show up, but emotionally she had held a silent but fervent wish that he'd swoop in, haul her into his arms, and kiss her senseless. He would say that after sorting things through, cooling his temper, he'd come to realize he'd been wrong and would she please, please, please ride off into the sunset with him?

Lux plunked her elbow on the desk, and rested her chin in her hand. So much for that lovely scenario, she mused.

"Okay," she said, smacking the desk with her hand. "Fine." She'd had enough of this stubborn Mullaney nonsense. It was time for action. And it would help immensely if she knew what to do. She had absolutely no idea how to . . .

Unless . . .

She stiffened in her chair as a plan began to slowly take shape in her mind. A smile formed on her lips, then grew bigger.

"Bingo!" she said brightly, then reached for the telephone.

Patrick sat in his den and pushed the button

on the remote control, changing the stations on the television in rapid succession. With a mumbled expletive, he turned off the set and drummed his fingers on the arm of the leather chair.

He was bored, tense, edgy, and in a rotten mood. And he missed Lux Sherwood. It was Friday afternoon of the longest, most miserable week of his life. What kind of week had Lux had, he wondered. Had she cried? Thought of him? Missed him as much as he had her? Hell, he didn't care. Not at all.

Lux had sat in her living room and admitted that he was nothing more than a replacement for Mick and the others. She had known all along, Patrick fumed on, that she needed to be needed, was aware of her ghosts, and was using him to fill a void in her existence. That wasn't love in its proper place, real and honest, between a man and a woman. He wanted no part of what Lux was offering him.

But he missed her.

By merely closing his eyes he could see her, hear her laughter and the soft sounds she purred when he made love with her. Exquisite love, like none he had ever known before. He could see her shiny, dark hair swinging around her beautiful face, could even fill his senses with her special aroma.

He loved her. He ached for her. And he was cut to the quick by her deception.

Patrick sighed deeply. He was tired, hadn't slept well all week, but his knee was doing fine. He should be planning his future, but he lacked the enthusiasm to seriously consider any of the offers being made to him. He couldn't go on like this. He knew it, but all he could think about now was Lux.

"Hell," he said.

The doorbell rang.

"Hell," he repeated, as he remembered that Maria was away visiting her daughter.

He leveled himself up, and walked from the room, determined to get rid of whoever was on the other side of the door. He flung open the wooden panel, then his eyes widened.

Standing before him was a six-foot, furry, pink teddy bear!

And a pair of big, blue eyes were peering at him from beneath the bear's arm.

Lux! Patrick thought wildly. What in the hell was she up to? Lux was there! His beautiful, wonderful Lux was . . . No! No, dammit, he didn't want her here with her phony love, her . . .

"Mr. Mullaney?" came a muffled voice.

"What? Yeah. Look, I don't . . ."

"Mr. Teddy Mullaney?"

"Huh?"

"It's imperative that I see Teddy Mullaney, sir. May I come in?"

No! "Yes," Patrick heard himself say. He stepped back to allow the pink bear and its keeper to enter.

"Thank you," the voice said. "May we see Teddy, please?"

"Oh, what the hell, why not?" Patrick said, throwing up his hands. What was she up to! "Go in the den. I'll get Teddy."

"You're ever so kind."

"Mmm," Patrick said darkly, then turned and went down the hall.

In the den, Lux heaved the big, smiling bear onto the sofa, then drew a steadying breath.

Patrick looked so tired, so angry, and she loved

him so much. This had to work she told herself, it just had to. The hours of the week had seemed endless as she'd waited for the pink bear to be finished. But this was it.

Patrick came into the room and plunked Teddy onto the sofa next to the pink bear.

"Spiffy outfit, Teddy," Lux said, glancing at the football jersey. She couldn't look at Patrick, not now, or she'd fall apart. "Teddy, you remember . . . Tammy here. Of course you do. She has missed you so much. The way you parted was very sad and very wrong. Tammy didn't have a chance to explain because you were so angry."

"Lux . . ." Patrick started.

Lux ignored him and rushed on. "Teddy, listen, please listen." Oh, Lord, she was going to cry. No, she mustn't cry! Not now. "My love . . . I mean, Tammy's love for you is real, it's honest, it's every bit as true as yours is for her. I know you love her, Teddy. I'll never believe otherwise."

Lux swallowed past the lump in her throat. "Teddy, Tammy didn't use you. She was confused, muddled, but then she remembered some important, beautiful words her Gran had spoken to her many years ago. Tammy faced the ghosts, the unhealthy need to be needed, the truth of how she'd surrounded herself with people who needed her."

Two tears slid unnoticed down Lux's face. "She did battle with the ghosts, Teddy, while you were away. And she won. And, Teddy?" A sob escaped from her lips. "She knew that her love for you was real, was forever, had always been separate and apart, in a special, warm fuzzy place, from where the ghosts were."

"Lux, I . . ."

"Please, Teddy?" she said, sobbing openly. "Please believe Tammy? Don't throw away all that you have together. Please?"

With a strangled moan, Patrick grabbed Lux, turned her to him, and pulled her tightly into his arms. He buried his face in her fragrant, silky hair. She rested her head on his chest, trying to stop her flow of tears, her breathing an unsteady rush of air. Patrick wove his fingers through her hair, and tilted her head back to meet his gaze.

"Oh, Lux," he said, his voice husky with emotion, "I'm sorry, so damn sorry. I realize now that I didn't give you a chance to explain on Sunday night. I just came barreling in there, and you said . . . and I thought . . . and I was so damn hurt, just blown away. I love you, Lux, and I've ached with missing you, wanting you."

"Oh, Patrick, you knew about my ghosts before I did. That told me how much you loved me, gave me the courage to come here. I love you so very much."

"Forgive me, please, for not listening, for not believing in you."

"Patrick, I love you, I want you, and . . ." She drew a deep breath. ". . . I need you. I need you, Patrick 'Acer' Mullaney, the way a woman in love needs her man, her partner, her other half, next to her through the good times and bad."

"And *I* need you," he said, his voice breaking. Tears shimmered in his eyes. "Will you marry me, Lux Sherwood? Will you come to Switzerland with me on our honeymoon? Then be by my side as I choose my future career? Will you be my wife, my life, the mother of my baby? Please, Lux?"

"Oh, yes," she said, smiling through her tears. "Oh, Patrick, yes!"

He claimed her mouth in a hard, searing kiss that gentled as the agonizing memories of the past week were swept into oblivion.

"I want to make love with you," he said, close to her lips. "Now."

"Yes."

Patrick circled Lux's shoulders with his arm and tucked her close to his side as they started across the room. At the doorway he stopped and looked back at Teddy.

"That's quite a woman you've got there in Tammy, Teddy," he said. "Don't blow it, buddy. Love like this only comes along once in a lifetime."

Lux looked up at Patrick, the message of love clear in her eyes. He met her gaze, then they left the room. They headed down the hall to the bedroom, anticipating what they would share. It would be only the two of them, but together they were the universe, all and everything. And in love.

In the den, as though moved by an invisible hand, Tammy tilted over, her head coming to rest on Teddy's shoulder.

The furry pink and blue bears were smiling.

THE EDITOR'S CORNER

We sail into our LOVESWEPT summer with six couples who, at first glance, seem to be unlikely matches. What they all have in common, and the reason that everything works out in the end, is Cupid's arrow. When true love strikes, there's no turning back—not for Shawna and Parker, her fiance, who doesn't even remember that he's engaged; not for Annabella and Terry, who live in completely different worlds; not for Summer and Cabe, who can't forget their teenage love. Holly and Steven were never meant to fall in love—Holly was supposed to get a juicy story, not a marriage proposal, from the famous bachelor. And our last two couples for the month are probably the most unlikely matches of all—strangers thrown together for a night who can't resist Cupid's arrow and turn an evening of romance into a lifetime of love!

We're very pleased to introduce Susan Crose to you this month. With **THE BRASS RING,** she's making her debut as a LOVESWEPT author—and what a sparkling debut it is! Be on the lookout for the beautiful cover on this book—it's our first bride and groom in a long time!

THE BRASS RING, LOVESWEPT #264, opens on the eve of Shawna McGuire's and Parker Harrison's wedding day when it seems that nothing can mar their perfect joy and anticipation on becoming husband and wife. But there's a terrible accident, and Shawna is left waiting at the church. Shawna almost loses her man, but she never gives up, and finally they do get to say their vows. This is a story about falling in love with the same person twice, and what could be more romantic than that?

Joan Elliott Pickart's **THE ENCHANTING MISS ANNA-BELLA,** LOVESWEPT #265, is such an enchanting love story that I guarantee you won't want to put this book down. Miss Annabella is the librarian in Harmony, Oklahoma, and Terry Russell is a gorgeous, blue-eyed, ladykiller pilot who has returned to the tiny town to visit his folks. All the ladies in Harmony fantasize about handsome Terry Russell, but Annabella doesn't even know what a fantasy is! Annabella's a late bloomer, and Terry is the

(continued)

one who helps her to blossom. Terry sees the woman hidden inside, and he falls in love with her. Annabella discovers herself, and then she can return Terry's love. When that happens, it's a match made in heaven!

FLYNN'S FATE, by Patt Bucheister, LOVESWEPT #266, is another example of this author's skill in touching our emotions. Summer Roberts loves the small town life and doesn't trust Cabe Flynn, the city slicker who lives life in Chicago's fast lane. Cabe was her teenage heartthrob, but years ago he gave up on Clearview and on Summer. Now he's back to claim his legacy, and Summer finds she can't bear to spend time with him because he awakens a sweet, wild hunger in her. Cabe wants to explore the intense attraction between them; he won't ignore his growing desire. He knows his own mind, and he also knows that Summer is his destiny—and with moonlight sails and words of love, he shows her this truth.

In **MADE FOR EACH OTHER** by Doris Parmett, LOVE-SWEPT #267, it's our heroine Holly Anderson's job to get an exclusive interview from LA's most eligible bachelor. Steven Chadwick guards his privacy so Holly goes undercover to get the scoop. She has no problem getting to know the gorgeous millionaire—in fact, he becomes her best friend and constant companion. Steven is too wonderful for words, and too gorgeous to resist, and Holly knows she must come clean and risk ruining their relationship. When friendly hugs turn into sizzling embraces, Holly gives up her story to gain his love. Best friends become best lovers! Doris Parmett is able to juggle all the elements of this story and deliver a wonderfully entertaining read.

STRICTLY BUSINESS by Linda Cajio, LOVESWEPT #268, maybe should have been titled, "Strictly Monkey Business". That describes the opening scene where Jess Brannen and Nick Mikaris wake up in bed together, scarcely having set eyes on each other before! They are both victims of a practical joke.

Things go from bad to worse when Jess shows up for a job interview and finds Nick behind the desk. They can't seem to stay away from each other, and Nick can't
(continued)

forget his image of her in that satin slip! Jess keeps insisting that she won't mix business with pleasure, even when she has the pleasure of experiencing his wildfire kisses. She doth protest too much—and finally her "no" becomes a "yes." This is Linda Cajio's sixth book for LOVESWEPT, and I know I speak for all your fans when I say, "Keep these wonderful stories coming, Linda!"

One of your favorite LOVESWEPT authors, Helen Mittermeyer, has a new book this month, and it's provocatively—and appropriately!—titled **ABLAZE**, LOVESWEPT #269. Heller Blane is a stunning blond actress working double shifts because she's desperately in need of funds. But is she desperate enough to accept $10,000 from a mysterious stranger *just* to have dinner with him? Conrad Wendell is dangerously appealing, and Heller is drawn to him. When their passionate night is over, she makes her escape, but Conrad cannot forget her. He's fallen in love with his vanished siren—she touched his soul—and he won't be happy until she's in his arms again. Thank you, Helen, for a new LOVESWEPT. **ABLAZE** has set our hearts on fire!

The HOMETOWN HUNK CONTEST is coming! We promised you entry blanks this month, but due to scheduling changes, the contest will officially begin next month. Just keep your eyes open for the magnificent men in your own hometown, then learn how to enter our HOMETOWN HUNK CONTEST *next month*.

Happy reading!

Sincerely,

Carolyn Nichols

Carolyn Nichols
  Editor
LOVESWEPT
Bantam Books
666 Fifth Avenue
New York, NY 10103

THE DELANEY DYNASTY

Men and women whose loves and passions are so glorious it takes many great romance novels by three bestselling authors to tell their tempestuous stories.

THE SHAMROCK TRINITY